DEFEN
OF MAI- UN

A STORY OF THE ROMAN
ASSAULT ON MAIDEN CASTLE

DAVID MACPHERSON

Roving
Press

© 2010 David Macpherson
Published by Roving Press Ltd
4 Southover Cottages, Frampton, Dorset, DT2 9NQ, UK
Tel: +44 (0)1300 321531
www.rovingpress.co.uk

The rights of the author to be identified as the Author of this Work
have been asserted in accordance with the Copyright, Designs and
Patents Act 1988.

All rights reserved. No part of this publication may be reproduced,
stored in a retrieval system or transmitted, in any form or by
any means, electronic, mechanical, photocopying or otherwise,
without the prior permission of the publisher.

This is a work of fiction. The characters, incidents and dialogues
are products of the author's imagination and are not to be
construed as real. Any resemblance to actual events or persons,
living or dead, is entirely coincidental.

First published 2010 by Roving Press Ltd
ISBN: 978-1-906651-08-4

British Library Cataloguing in Publication Data
A catalogue record for this book is available from the British
Library

Cover design by Roving Press
Cover illustrations by Paul Birkbeck © English Heritage
'Boy and sheep' drawing and map based on original artwork by
Keith Whittock

Set in Minion 11.5/13pt by www.beamreachuk.co.uk
Printed and bound by Rzeszowskie Zaklady Graficzne S.A. Poland.

To my wife Sue and children Anthony, Fiona and Charlotte, without whose unstinting encouragement this book would never have been completed.

BACKGROUND

In AD 41 Claudius became Emperor in Rome, succeeding his nephew Caligula who was murdered by disaffected army officers. Immediately after the murder, Claudius was lucky to escape with his life, but the Praetorian Guards protected him. To keep the army happy Claudius planned the invasion of Britain.

In AD 43 a force of four legions, under the overall command of Aulus Plautius, landed in Britain. The Second Legion was led by General Titus Flavius Vespasianus, future Emperor Vespasian. The legions defeated the native Celts at the battle of the River Medway in Kent. Aulus Plautius moved cautiously north but was held up at the River Thames. Uncertain what to do next he sent for the Emperor Claudius, who arrived 2 months later accompanied by 46 elephants. The Celts melted away and in 16 days, without needing to strike a blow, Claudius accepted the surrender of 16 kings and the town of Colchester, renamed *Camulodunum* by the Romans, which he made his capital. He then returned to Rome where the Senate gave him the title *Britannicus* and awarded him a triumph.

Vespasian was sent with the Second Legion to conquer Hampshire and in AD 44 successfully defeated the Atrebates who lived there. His legion went into winter quarters, mostly at Chichester (*Noviomagus*) with some on the Isle of Wight (*Vectis*). The Second Legion had been founded by the Emperor Augustus and named the *Augusta* after him. At full strength a Roman legion had nearly 6,000 men, divided into six cohorts, each with six centuries, each commanded by a centurion. The most important centurion was the *Primus Pilus* or Senior Spear who commanded the First Century and the First Cohort. In practice there were seldom more than 80 men in each century and it is likely that Vespasian's Augusta had around 4,800 legionaries in Dorset. Auxiliaries, cavalrymen and archers, drawn from conquered native tribes, supported each legion. When Vespasian was the General in command (*Legatus Legionis*), his elder brother Titus served with him. The third in command with the title *Praefectus Castrorum* or Camp Prefect was a very experienced officer called Maximus. Tribunes were officers with no specific military responsibility, to be used at the discretion of the General.

CHARACTERS

Romans

Claudius – Emperor of Rome
Aulus Plautius – Army Commander, First Governor of Britain
Vespasian – Commander of the II Legion (Augusta), future Emperor
Titus – Vespasian's elder brother
Maximus – Prefect of the Camp
Julius Graecinus – Tribune
Carinus – *Primus Pilus* or Senior Spear
Gaius – Senior Tribune
Vitellius – centurion
Novak and **Goran** – two soldiers, bodyguards to Vespasian
Rufius – naval captain
Drusus – tribune
Quintus – officer in command of Clavinium or Radipole Camp
Alexis – Greek slave and trained surveyor

Durotriges

Bannoc – Chieftain of Mai-dun
Garth – Celtic army commander
Maddoc – Druid known as the Teacher
Conn – young orphan boy
Kareth and **Gwillam** – old couple who Conn lives with
Rolf – Captain of the Slingers
Silda – Rolf's wife
Huw – Conn's friend and eldest son of Rolf
Morwen – Conn's girl friend and daughter of Rolf
Dirk and **Dug** – twin sons of Rolf
Serap, Bran, Brendan (Ox), Rodden – young soldiers, Huw's friends
Rohan – stranger from Hod

Place Names

Roman

Morionium – Wareham
Vectis – Isle of Wight
Durnovaria – Dorchester
Richborough – old Roman port of Richborough in Kent
Clavinium or **Reed Pool** – Radipole near Weymouth
White Rings – Badbury Rings near Wimborne
The Beak – Portland Bill
Great Lagoon – Poole
Lagoon Harbour – Hamworthy
Lake Camp – legionary fort at Lake Farm near Wimborne
Noviomagus – Chichester

Celtic

Mai-dun – Maiden Castle, Celtic hillfort
Durotriges – tribe living in modern Dorset
Atrebates – tribe inhabiting modern Hampshire
Dumnonii – tribe living in modern Devon
Venitii – tribe inhabiting Brittany in France
Isca Stour – Powerful Water (River Stour)
Isca Frome – Fair Water (River Frome)
Hod – Hod Hill, Celtic hillfort
Ham – Hambledon Hill, Celtic hillfort

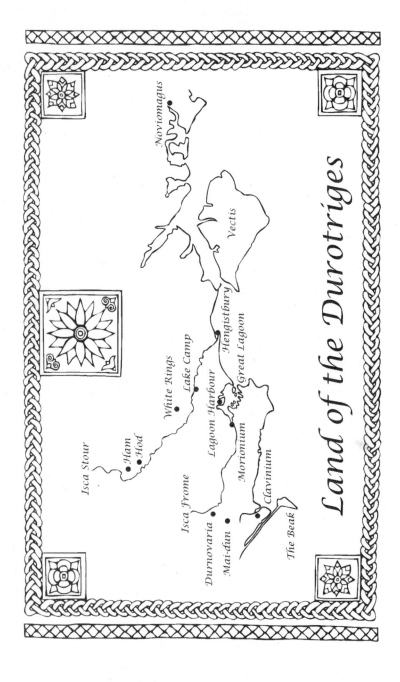

Land of the Durotríges

Noviomagus

Vectis

Isca Stour

Ham
Hod

White Rings

Lake Camp

Hengistbury

Great Lagoon

Lagoon Harbour

Isca Frome

Mortonium

Durnovaria

Mai-dun

Clavinium

The Beak

Chapter 1
MAI-DUN

The old woman was called Kareth, but Conn always thought of her as the old woman. She was small, mean and miserable. When Conn was around 3 years old, his village had been attacked and ransacked by a raiding party. His parents had been killed and the boy had been brought back as a trophy to the raiders' settlement of Mai-dun. The chieftain Bannoc had given him to the childless Kareth and her husband Gwillam and since then Conn had lived in a corner of their hut as their unpaid servant. He hated both of them for their casual cruelty. For nearly 12 years he had lived with them and slaved for them and he ached for the time, not so long now, when he could escape from their indifferent care.

'Get a move on you lazy lout,' Kareth turned to shout at Conn. 'If we don't get back before dark the gates will be shut and we'll have to spend the night outside the settlement.' Conn was 14 or 15 years old, he didn't know which. Anyhow he was small for his age and slightly built. His toughness was all inside. The ewe he was carrying over his shoulders had a broken leg, was heavy and was struggling to escape. In her fright she had pissed down the side of his smock, but this made little difference to the boy who lived his life in dirt. He gripped her three good legs tighter and shrugged the ewe higher on his back, bending forward under her weight. He was used to Kareth's insults by now and trudged forward in sullen silence. He knew from past experience that any reaction from him would result in a beating from Gwillam when he got home. Underneath the grime Conn had a handsome face, but he took care to keep it blank and expressionless. Inside he seethed with resentment and planned revenge, though he knew he could not escape this drudgery until he was past his 15th birthday. At that age under tribal law he was eligible to become a warrior. He could leave Kareth and Gwillam's household and move into a hut with the other young men. The Chief had told Kareth his birthday would be the summer solstice. Until then he must keep quiet.

Conn wore a simple threadbare tunic made of coarsely woven wool. Now soiled by the injured ewe, this tunic was tied by a piece of twisted rope round his waist. The leather sandals on his feet were worn and too small for him. The old woman in front of him cursed at the rest of the flock and drove them towards the hillfort that was their home. They would need to travel right round the foot of the hill, as Conn knew that the western gate would already be closed. The huge ramparts of Mai-dun were not far off, but Bannoc's rules were clear. When the sun set, the eastern gate would also be shut and the gateman was not to allow anyone to enter.

It was not Conn's fault that the ewe had broken her leg. The flock belonged to the community and that day Conn and the old woman had the responsibility of looking after them. They had driven the 40 sheep to the winter pasture early that morning. In plenty of time they had rounded them up to return home, but one silly animal had split from the rest and tried to run across the stream. Her front leg had slipped between two rocks and been trapped. For some time Conn and the old woman had pulled and shoved to get it free and when at last they managed it, the leg was obviously broken. A breeding ewe was valuable property for the people and could not be abandoned to the wolves so Kareth ordered Conn to carry her back to Mai-dun.

She thought perhaps Bannoc would not be too angry with them if they brought the injured animal home safely.

Mai-dun was the biggest of the hillforts of the Durotriges tribe which Kareth and Gwillam belonged to. Just under a thousand people lived on the huge grassy plateau in security behind the three massive banks of walls and ditches that surrounded the hill. At much the same time as Conn had been brought as a nameless child to join the community, Bannoc and his friends had arrived from somewhere overseas. They had moved into the settlement and had quickly become authorities. They brought a greater discipline and order over what had been a casual and disorganised community. Now Bannoc was the most feared chieftain for many miles around and Mai-dun was the unofficial capital of the area. Neither Kareth nor Conn wanted to risk Bannoc's anger. As the little group struggled around the north walls, Conn thought how he could easily have sneaked into the settlement, if he had been on his own, by one of the secret paths he and his friends had discovered through the defences. Fortunately Gwillam had warned the gateman that the old woman, Conn and the sheep were on their way and they drove their charges up the eastern causeway just in time. 'I won't wait for you another time,' he grumbled as the two huge wooden doors swung closed behind Conn.

3

'Shut the sheep away for the night,' the old woman shouted at Conn as she turned off the causeway with Gwillam to go to their hut. Conn laid the injured sheep on the grass, tied her back legs together to stop her escaping and rounded up the others. He drove them into the stockade where they would be secure behind the thorny fence. He then collected water from the dew pond to fill their wooden trough for the night and went back to the injured ewe. He hoisted her onto his shoulders once more and, going back to the enclosure, left her with the others. Having safely bedded down all the sheep he trudged wearily back to the hut he shared with the old woman and her husband.

Conn pushed aside a tattered piece of material, which acted as the door screen to their hut. Inside it was gloomy and stark. Kareth and Gwillam lived in one of the smallest round houses and neither noticed the dirt. The hut was devoid of decoration and Conn's place was a pile of straw against one wall. The room was filled with smoke and the old woman was sitting by the fire stirring something in a pot. Conn was looking forward to some food and sleep, but Kareth had still more for him to do. 'Go and report the sheep's injury to Bannoc,' she said. 'I'll not have him finding out about your mistakes from gossip.'

Conn knew where Bannoc's hut was, but he had never been in it, nor had he ever spoken to the Chief. By now it was dark, but he walked confidently enough up the main central path until he came to the biggest hut. He heard laughter from inside and, his confidence seeping away, he nervously stepped in through the doorway. By the dim light provided by the rush lamps Conn could see five or six men sitting around the fire on log benches. He recognised Bannoc in the middle. The Chief was a huge man whose presence dominated the room. His long golden hair curled at the shoulder and his full beard was shiny with animal fat. He was half-turned towards the man next to him, listening

4

intently to what was being said. In front of him, Bannoc's woman was bending over the clay oven and pulling out some bread she had been baking. Conn shrank back in the doorway anxious not to disturb the gathering, undecided what to do. He knew well the old man on Bannoc's left, the one who was speaking. This was Maddoc, the seer. In some villages Maddoc would be called a Druid, but in Maidun he was known as the Teacher. Conn frequently went to Maddoc's hut to help him with his chores. The old man was reciting verse, which told the story of a white bird and a faraway land. Conn did not really understand the poem, but when it was finished those present cheered and clapped as if they had enjoyed it. Bannoc poured some beer into one of the pottery mugs and handed it to Maddoc. On Bannoc's right was Rolf, Captain of the Slingers. Rolf lived in a hut near to Conn and was the father of his best friend Huw and also Morwen and the twins Dirk and Dug. Conn liked Rolf but was also a little afraid of him. Rolf noticed Conn standing in the shadows and drew Bannoc's attention to him. The Chief beckoned him forward. 'Come here. What is it, boy?'

Conn shuffled forward. 'One of the ewes from the north pasture broke her leg today.'

'Where is she now?' the Chieftain asked.

'I carried her back and left her in the pen,' answered Conn. There was a look of approval on the faces of those round the fire. The men recognised the effort that must have been put in bringing the wounded sheep home from such a distance.

'How old is the animal?' Bannoc continued his questioning.

'Kareth says she thinks she's about 5 years old.'

There was some muttering from those round the fire and Bannoc came to his decision. 'She will not be much good for breeding after 5 years. Take her to the slaughterer in the morning and tell him I want some mutton stew tomorrow night.' The dead sheep would feed more than just Bannoc. Many of the inhabitants would benefit because Conn had carried the animal home. 'All right lad,' Bannoc waved Conn away, 'you can go now.'

Conn hesitated in the doorway. He wanted to put a question to Bannoc, but his nerve deserted him. Maddoc noticed that Conn had not yet left the Chief's hut and, leaning across the table, he whispered something to Bannoc. The Chief nodded and looked at the waiting boy. 'Conn is it? Well, Conn, the skin is yours. I think you've earned it.'

Conn ran back to his hut glowing with pleasure. To wear a sheepskin over-jacket was usually the privilege of a warrior. The adults he knew wore skins from wolves and other wild animals. Village gossip said that Bannoc's magnificent coat was from a bear he had killed in Gaul many years ago. To Conn, permission to wear a sheepskin was the first sign of his changing status. He did not mind the insults and petty tasks he was given by Kareth before he went to bed. He was one step nearer to escaping from his drudgery.

Early next morning Conn avoided having to carry out the stream of instructions that came from Kareth by telling her he had to carry out orders for Bannoc. That quickly silenced the old woman. He carried the injured sheep to the slaughterer and passed on the message about the mutton stew. 'Who's to get the skin?' the man asked Conn.

'I am,' the boy answered proudly.

'Well, I'll have it ready for you by mid-morning,' said the man, seizing the struggling animal by one leg. 'You'll have to cure it yourself.'

Conn ran off to find his friend. Huw was outside Mai-dun's defences practising with his sling. Conn got out his own leather straps and the two friends spent some time slinging pebbles at various posts and bushes. Huw, at 16, had been in the defence force for over a year, but Conn thought that this was mainly because Rolf, his father, was Captain of the Slingers. He was at least a year older and a foot taller than Conn and fair-haired like all his family. Conn liked him because he was always smiling and cheerful and took no account of their different status. Huw was impressed how much Conn's skill had improved and told him so. Conn had been practising hard and grinned at his friend's compliment. 'I will tell father how good you have become,' Huw said. Conn proudly explained to him about the sheepskin. Well before midday the two boys waited impatiently outside the slaughterer's hut.

'The head and hooves are always mine', the man explained through the open doorway. 'Here's your bit.' He threw the skin out to them. 'Boy, you take this to your mother.' He handed a bloody lump of meat to Huw.

Conn picked up the sheepskin and as he was about to leave just remembered to ask the man, 'How do I cure it?'

'Cheapest and easiest is ox piss,' came the reply, 'though I prefer to rub it with salt.' Grudgingly the man gave in to the boys' pleadings and agreed to give them a precious handful of salt and the two of them hurried off. In a small grassy hollow by the back of Conn's hut they pinned the skin out on the ground using sticks from the woodpile. Under the eaves of the house Huw found a tool made from an oxen's shoulder blade and the two friends took it in turns carefully to scrape off most of the bits of flesh. They then rubbed the salt crystals into the leather. Standing back to admire their work Conn asked Huw anxiously, 'How long do we have to leave it for?'

'I've never done it before,' Huw answered, scratching his head. 'About a week probably.'

'I can't wait that long, I want to show it ...' Conn stopped mid sentence and finished rather lamely, 'I want to show it.'

'You want to show it to Morwen,' teased Huw. Conn's blush showed that his friend had hit the mark. Morwen, Huw's sister, was the same age as Conn, and to him she was the most beautiful girl in the world. The two had grown up together and it was she who, with gentle humour, had first coaxed a smile from the sullen child he used to be. With Morwen, Conn was not silent and tongue-tied and over the years she had slowly trained him away from the savage behaviour he had learned living with Kareth and Gwillam. At 14 it was still to her that Conn brought all his treasures. Rolf had watched the friendship between his daughter and the no-named foundling with amused tolerance. Soon, when the time came for his daughter to wed, she would marry someone worthy of his family's status. Until then she would come to no harm being befriended by Conn.

That evening Conn unpinned the sheepskin from the ground where it had been stretched and cut a slit in the centre with his knife. He put it over his head and held it fast round his waist with a leather belt lent to him by Huw. He walked the short distance to Rolf's house with a bit of a swagger in his step. Rolf was not in, but his wife Silda, who had always been kind to Conn, welcomed him. She felt sorry for the condition of his life in the squalid hut next door. At first she had looked out for him due to pity, but over the years she had come to recognise in the strange, silent boy a spark of something out of the ordinary that intrigued her. 'Huw's not here at the moment,' she said, ushering him in, 'but come and have some food.'

The hut where Rolf and Silda lived with their four children was a good deal bigger and much neater than the miserable place in which Conn lived with the old couple. There were animal skins on the floor and bunches of herbs and berries hanging from the roof timbers. The adults slept on a raised platform round one side of the hut and the children slept on rush mats round the other sides. All the mud walls had been decorated with simple drawings. Because the roof had been recently thatched with new reeds and was much higher than Conn's hut the house was far less smoky. Silda handed Conn a bowl with some stew in it. *Probably the sheep I brought back yesterday*, thought Conn. Just then Rolf came into the hut and the family shuffled around to make room for everyone. Conn found himself sitting next to Morwen. Dirk and Dug, her 8-year-old twin brothers, were sitting on the other side of the hearth scraping the food out of their wooden bowls with their fingers. Conn had often visited in the past, but on this occasion he was self-consciously aware that the sheepskin had changed his status.

'Nice coat', Rolf said.

Conn blurted out that one day he hoped to join the slingers. 'I practise every day,' he said and fell awkwardly silent.

'You can't be considered until you've turned 15. That's our rule. Bannoc has decided that'll be in the summer,' Rolf said firmly though not unkindly. 'In the meantime, work hard for Kareth and Gwillam.'

With the heat from the fire Conn was becoming aware that a strong smell of sheep was coming from his coat. He wished he had listened to Huw's advice about taking a week to cure the hide. Dirk and Dug began rolling their eyes and holding their noses. Morwen, laughing, stroked his new jacket. Conn smiled self-consciously. 'I think the coat is wonderful,' she said, 'but just for now why don't you take it off and leave it outside?' Conn was relieved to do so. Huw returned soon after and they all spent a relaxed evening chatting and playing dice round the hearth by the flickering firelight, until it was time for Conn to return to his own cold bed.

Chapter 2
WINTER QUARTERS

'Dispatches for the General; dispatches for the General.' The shout was repeated by each of the guards in turn. The soldier guarding the door of the officers' quarters pushed it open, entered and saluted. 'Messenger arrived from Rome, Sir.'

Titus Flavius Vespasianus, Legate in command of the Second Legion, the Augusta, was a tall man with strong square features. Today was his 33rd birthday, but, with his greying hair, he looked older and he certainly did not feel like celebrating. His legion was in winter quarters at Chichester on the mainland after the swift and ruthless campaign of conquest of the island of Vectis. The Roman army had returned to Britain the previous summer after an absence of 90 years and Vespasian was worried that he had been shuffled aside in an unimportant corner of Britain while others were achieving glory elsewhere. He put down the stylus he had been using and looked up. 'Send him in, soldier,' he commanded and he stood up, adjusting his cloak. He turned to his companion in the tent who was stretched out on a couch. 'At last we will find out what is to happen to us,' Vespasian said. 'An army could rot away on this God-forsaken coast.'

The man lying on the couch was Titus Sabinus, Vespasian's second-in-command and his older brother. Titus was much more easy-going than his younger brother and not so ambitious. Many older brothers would have been jealous of the other's success, but not Titus. He worked comfortably under his younger sibling's command, happily recognising Vespasian's brilliance. The two had fought side by side for 3 years, first in Germany and most recently in the bloody battle at the crossing of the River Medway. There Titus had proved himself a fearless leader and had personally rescued his brother when barbarian warriors had tried to drown him. But an army in winter quarters could be a miserable thing and the mercurial Vespasian would often find himself overwhelmed by doubts. At these moments he was grateful to his brother for his constant, cheerful optimism. Titus sat up excitedly. 'I believe this is the moment we have waited for, brother. The Augusta is ready and so are you.'

'Caution, Titus,' replied Vespasian. 'One or both of us could easily be recalled to Rome, or the Augusta might be sent to Colchester to join Plautius in his thrust north.'

A young man, around 22 years old, entered the tent and, standing in front of Vespasian, saluted. He was covered in mud and grey with fatigue. 'To Titus Flavius Vespasianus, Commander of the Emperor's own Second Legion, from his Imperial Majesty Claudius Caesar Augustus, greetings.' He saluted again.

'Sit down, man. You must be exhausted,' said Vespasian, and the soldier gratefully lowered himself onto the nearest stool. 'Have something to drink,' and without waiting for a reply the General shouted for his servant to bring some wine. 'What is your name?'

The young man scrambled back to his feet and bringing his fist sharply across his chest in salute answered 'Julius Graecinus, Tribune of the Fourth Legion, Sir.'

'Sit down, Tribune Graecinus, and try to relax. There's no need to be so formal just now. You will tire us both out with all that saluting. The Augusta has been camped here for 2 months, it's raining and we are not going anywhere in a hurry. Now tell me about yourself and your journey.'

Julius carefully sat down, a little nervous. He was an

imperial messenger and as such had an important status, but he recognised the obvious aura of authority that came from Vespasian. He was about to answer when the house servant brought in a mug of wine and offered it to Julius. He took a grateful swig and some of the tension left him. He straightened himself up and began to give his report.

'After 2 years with the Fourth Legion in Gaul, I was appointed to the imperial staff in Rome. My father is Senator Graecinus and he bought me the rank of Tribune. But I am anxious to see some active service and so I volunteered for this duty. I saw the Emperor himself at the end of October and he ordered me to find you and deliver dispatches. His Majesty's freed man, Narcissus, handed me these,' he said, drawing from under his cloak the leather pouch carried by all imperial messengers. He laid it on the table. 'Narcissus ordered me to make sure I gave them to no one but you.'

Titus sat up on the couch smiling. 'If these are orders from Narcissus it's bound to be good news.' He stretched out his hand to the table to take the travel-stained pouch.

Vespasian put his hand on the wallet and said quietly, 'Not yet, brother. Go on with your story, Tribune.'

'I was accompanied by another tribune, Marcus Gallus, who has orders for His Excellency Governor Plautius in Colchester. We took ship from Ostia and had an easy voyage to Marseilles in southern Gaul. From there we relayed our horses and rode as fast as we could to Brest on the north-west coast. I had been stationed there with the Fourth Legion for the last 2 years and know northern Gaul well. I learned to speak the language of the Venitii people so I was able to charter a small fishing boat from Brest and sail to Richborough. There Tribune Gallus and I separated and it has taken me two further days to reach your camp, Sir.'

Vespasian smiled with pleasure. This was the sort of officer that made the Roman army so powerful. 'An excellent journey. In total, how many days since you left Rome?'

'Altogether 21 days, Sir, including one day in Brest as we bargained for our voyage.'

'You have done well.' The General stood up. He was a tall man and towered over the young tribune. 'I shall make sure it is recorded in the register that you have served your Emperor well. Now, go and find the deputy to the Camp Prefect and he will make sure you are looked after.'

Julius rose from his stool but hesitated to leave. He was nervous about the next part of his orders, not knowing how it would be received. He looked straight at Vespasian. 'The Emperor also gave me a message I was to give to you in person, Sir.' He looked across at Titus who was still lounging on the couch. 'Alone, Sir, to you only.'

Vespasian looked severely at Julius. 'Soldier, do you know who this is?' He indicated Titus. 'This man is Titus Flavius Sabinus, my second-in-command and my brother. I have no secrets from him. Now go and have a bath, put on some fresh clothes and then give me and my brother Claudius's private message when you return in half an hour. In the meantime we will see what Rome has to tell us.' Julius saluted, turned and left the hut.

'How intriguing,' said Titus. 'I wonder what the old goat wants you to know that he can't put in dispatches.'

Vespasian frowned and put his finger to his lips. 'Careful, brother. I know the soldiers of the Augusta would not betray either of us, but I am aware that Plautius has agents in this camp and if your remarks were to get back to Rome ...' He shrugged his shoulders. He picked up the leather pouch, inspected the imperial seal to ensure it was still intact and broke it. Two scrolls and a letter spilled out onto the table. Vespasian broke the seal on the first scroll and quickly read through the document. He handed it over to his brother. 'This is just the official confirmation of my command from the Senate dated weeks ago. *Strategic orders will be given by the appropriate authority,* he read.

'I expect they are still not quite sure about you.' Titus

smiled. 'They want to make certain you don't get too big for your boots. Things are not completely secure in Rome yet, and the Flavian family has no-one there who could be held as a hostage for our good behaviour.'

Vespasian opened the second scroll and carefully read it from top to bottom. 'I think this is what we've been waiting for,' he said. '*The Second Legion is ordered to confront the Durotriges and the Dumnonii and to defeat them.*' He handed the scroll to his brother. 'We are to secure the whole of the south coast of Britannia and to make sure that all trade routes are in the hands of Rome. The supplies for this campaign are to come from Gaul and we are given complete authority, under the overall command of Governor Plautius, naturally, to achieve this.' Vespasian stood up and hugged his brother. 'An independent command at last. At least I think it is, though I am not sure what the last sentence in Claudius's letter means. Perhaps his private message will explain all.'

Titus picked up the sealed letter that was still lying on the table and held it to his nose. 'From Domitilla I believe.' He smiled at his brother and said, 'I will go and have a bath while you read what my sister-in-law writes of the gossip from Rome. I will come back in time to hear what message our young tribune has to report to us.'

Vespasian settled back on the couch as his brother left the tent, broke open the seal of his private letter and started to read. Half an hour later when Titus came back to the tent, Vespasian, now completely relaxed, was asleep on the couch with the letter lying on his chest. Titus shook him awake. 'What is the real news from Rome, brother?' he asked.

Vespasian looked serious for a moment. 'Well, apples have never been more expensive than they are now, and your niece, little Doma, has her first cold of winter. Your name-sake, Titus, plays all the time with a wooden sword, running up and down the house shouting "Where are the barbarians?" like all 3-year-old Roman boys should. There is talk of a new aqueduct for the city and ... Domitilla is well.' He did not add that she wrote that she missed him, loved him and hoped daily for his return.

Right on time Julius re-entered the commander's tent. He had obviously bathed and found some fresh clothes from somewhere. He was looking and feeling more confident. Vespasian waved a hand towards a stool and Julius sat down. 'Now tell me, Graecinus, what is the private message from his Imperial Majesty that was for my ears alone?'

'Well, Sir, it was Narcissus who actually gave me the message, but Claudius, I mean his Imperial Majesty, told him to tell me to tell you ... if you see what I mean.' Vespasian nodded and encouraged by this Julius continued. 'The Senate awarded Claudius a military triumph in the City after his victory at Colchester and said he could add the title Britannicus to his name. The Emperor has never used it, I think because he feels he did little enough to earn it. He does call his son Britannicus because he wants Rome to know that the island of Britain is important to him. To keep funds coming for this campaign he needs victories, but he is not certain that His Excellency Governor Plautius will give him these. He feels that the commander was too cautious after the battle of the River Medway – the Emperor's instinct is that an immediate thrust across the River Thames could have brought a speedy end to the campaign. Although Plautius is still the Governor in Britain, you and the Augusta are to act independently with authority directly from the Emperor. That is why all your outside supplies will come directly from Gaul.' Julius stopped and swallowed nervously.

'Is that all?' Vespasian asked.

'No, Sir. After I left the Emperor, Narcissus came out with me. He told me to tell you he could guarantee you 3 years for this campaign. He would keep Plautius off your back for that time, that's his words not mine, Sir, and in return he wants you to secure the tin trade from the territory west of this mainland. This would guarantee funds for the future conquest of Britain.'

Vespasian looked thoughtfully at the young man sitting in front of him. As always he was quick to make a character assessment. 'Thank you, Tribune. You know things that perhaps you should not, but as Narcissus trusted you, so shall I. My written orders confirm that you are transferred to my command. You are now a member of the Second Legion, the very proud Augusta. You will have a position in the Second Cohort, but will act under my direct authority. Now go and find a place to sleep and report back to me tomorrow.' Julius saluted and left.

'Impressive young man,' Titus said thoughtfully. 'Even though the tribune is a political placeman, I like him. He seems to be honest and ambitious, I only hope for your sake he is also discreet.' He looked at his brother with a worried expression. 'I do not like the idea of secret orders. Don't you think we should ask for written clarification, or at least make sure that Plautius knows what we are doing?'

Vespasian leaped from the couch full of renewed energy. 'By Jupiter, this is what we have prayed for. I am not waiting any longer for further orders. If in 3 years we conquer southern Britain no-one will question whether our orders were in writing or not. If I and the Augusta cannot succeed here, I have no future in the army anyway.' He walked rapidly up and down the hut, excited by the possibilities the future might hold for him. Titus could see that any lethargy had gone and Vespasian's mind was firing with plans. 'Brother, can you report here tomorrow at first light and bring Maximus with you? Please leave me now. I have work to do.'

Chapter 3
THE GRAIN PIT

At 8 years old Dirk and Dug were expected to play their part in supporting the family, but pinning them down to do a job of work was not easy. The hours of daylight were short in early December and the long periods of winter darkness when families were cooped up in their huts like chickens were always difficult. For the twins, who had an excess of energy all year round, these evenings dragged on and their parents did their best to tire them out during the day. This morning Rolf had ordered them to collect firewood with the bribe that they would be free to play with their friends for the last few hours before dusk. Both boys were strong enough to carry a full load and they set off cheerfully enough with the necessary hatchet and leather and twine binders for the logs.

As they left their hut they passed Conn working on one of the community dew ponds. Bannoc insisted that everyone should take their turn doing work for the community. The old woman frequently passed her responsibilities on to Conn, complaining of ill-health, and today he was taking her place in the working party. One of the dew ponds had not been holding water that summer and the Elders had decided that it should be relined. Conn was working with two of the more ancient tribesmen, so much of the hard work fell on him. First they had drained the pond with buckets, and by the time Dirk and Dug saw Conn and called out to him, all three of the pond workers were shovelling as much of the sloppy mud as they could from the bottom of the hollow onto the grass. It was necessary to clear back to the original clay lining to see where the repairs should be made. The work was heavy and messy and Conn did not welcome the cheerful insults thrown at him by the twins. Like most members of Mai-dun he could not tell them apart, but it rarely mattered as they did everything together. Conn picked up a handful of mud and hurled it towards them. He scored a direct hit on either Dirk or Dug, but neither was dismayed and they both ran off with shrieks of laughter. Conn envied their irresponsibility.

Although both boys appeared carefree, they had a healthy respect for their father and mother and knew that if they failed in the job set for them they would be beaten. They worked hard in the morning collecting wood from the ash coppice near the winter bourn. The twins had each carried several good loads of logs back up onto the hill by mid-morning and when they staggered past Conn for the final time, neither of them had the breath to spare for shouting jibes. The boys arrived back home and Silda told them to stack the wood under the eaves of the hut. When they had done this they were free to go and play. Morwen was grinding corn inside and Dug whispered to her from the doorway, 'We saw your boy-friend working at the dew pond. He really is smelly now.' With that the boys ran off.

Early in the morning one of the tribesmen with an ox cart had left the hill to start collecting clay from the flood plain of the Frome river. This was necessary because there was no material suitable for the dew pond repairs in the chalk of Mai-dun. Throughout the morning the carter had returned many times, whipping his oxen up the flint-covered causeway into the settlement. Each time he drove the rough cart over to the dew pond and, without a word, tipped his load onto the ground. While his co-workers puddled the clay with their feet Conn smeared the result around the walls and base of the pond. There were eight dew ponds on Mai-dun, two were for cattle to drink from and the remainder for the people to use. Despite their name the dew ponds were primarily filled by rainwater. It was vital for the community during the months of summer, when the winter bourn was swallowed up by the chalk soil, that the ponds provided a reliable source of water. Conn smoothed the surface carefully, knowing he would be in trouble if his work was slapdash. He was beginning to feel his back aching and as he stood up to stretch he saw Morwen running franticly towards him. He scrambled up the side of the pond and went to meet her.

'Oh, Conn, come quickly,' she gasped.

Conn tried to calm her while she got her breath back. 'What's the matter?' he asked.

'Dirk has fallen into our grain pit. He was playing "Seek" with Dug and he must have found someone had forgotten to put the lid back on the pit. I suppose he thought it would be a good place to hide.' She grabbed his arm. 'Hurry!'

Together they ran towards Morwen's hut. She managed to explain, 'I was grinding corn at home when Dug rushed in white-faced. He couldn't speak. He tried to drag me to the door, but I was annoyed with him and shrugged him off. He started crying and eventually blurted out that Dirk was in trouble. That's quite usual, but he got more and more frantic so I went with him. He said Dirk was in the pit and ours is one of the biggest; as deep as two men. I was frightened what father would say, so I came to get you.'

The area of Mai-dun was riddled with pits dug into the chalk. Some were quite shallow and used for household debris, but the deepest were for storing grain. These could be up to 11 ft deep and all were waterproofed with clay. The grain pits were usually bell-shaped and the tops closed with a slab of stone and sealed tight with a mixture of clay and dung. This way the rye or oats could be kept dry for a whole year. If the seal was not broken grain could be kept for up to 5 years in some pits. Now, in December, most of the grain pits were full from this year's harvest. All the children knew that they were out of bounds to their games.

Morwen and Conn arrived breathless at the pit some way behind Rolf's house, where they found Dug kneeling on the ground, weeping uncontrollably. Conn picked him up and shook him. Dug stopped crying for a moment and pointed at the hole. The slab of stone had been moved aside and Conn threw himself down on the ground by the pit's entrance.

'Dirk, Dirk can you hear me?' he shouted. He stopped to listen. Nothing. He shouted again, and this time he heard a whimpering. 'Dirk, try not to move. I'm coming to help you.'

Conn knew that it was never safe to stand on the grain. There were stories of people falling into pits and suffocating to death, but Conn had always assumed these were just to frighten children. He had seen men lowered carefully into the pits when the level had sunk so low that the grain could not be drawn up in buckets. He ordered Morwen and Dug to go to the nearby huts and to collect as much rope as they could. If there was no rope, the leather traces for the oxen would do instead. As Morwen ran off, Conn shouted after her, 'I'm going to need some help too.' He lay back on the ground and put his head over the edge of the pit. As he leaned right over, he could see beyond the neck into the body of the bell.

'Dirk, listen. As soon as I have some rope I'm coming in to get you. Can you hear me?' There was a muffled 'Yes', and Conn reckoned he could see the outline of Dirk's face in the dark over against one wall of the pit.

Dug and Morwen arrived back with a tangle of ropes and harnesses that they had collected. With them came the man and woman from the next hut, attracted by the noise. 'Sort these ropes out,' Conn ordered, and Dug and Morwen started to straighten out some of the muddle. Conn quickly explained the situation to the man and his wife and told them what he needed from them. They disappeared into their hut, taking with them the longest rope. In a few moments this was passed through a gap in the wattle of their hut wall. Conn pulled on it and found it to be secure. He assumed it was tied to one of the roof posts of the hut as this was the usual practice for securing a rope.

Morwen had sorted out a length of leather harness, which Conn tied around his waist, and rapidly, with Dug's help, they unravelled sufficient lengths to reach the lip of the pit. Conn carefully tested each section for strength and then knotted them together. He then, just as carefully, tested each knot in turn and secured the end rope to his harness. The man had returned to help and Conn asked him to hold the rope and to lower him into the pit. More and more people were arriving to see what was happening and many shouted advice to Conn. But now he was concentrating on what he had to do next, and he shut himself off from the comments. He lowered his feet over the edge of the pit and was just about to transfer his weight onto the corn when the twins' mother, Silda, rushed over.

She had been visiting a sick friend when someone had passed on the news of Dirk's accident. She pushed her way through the small crowd and quickly realised what Conn was trying to do.

'Be careful, Conn,' was all she said as she stepped back into the crowd.

Very gently he lowered himself down. At first his footing seemed secure enough, but quickly he found his feet beginning to sink into the grain. He slackened off some more of the rope, pushing his feet out in front and shrugged himself into a lying position. With his weight spread evenly he found that he could stop sinking and, using his hands, he swam over the grain towards Dirk. The boy's head was only just above the surface of the corn and one arm was showing. Conn grabbed it and held on. It was important that Dirk did not panic at this point and Conn spoke quietly to calm him down. 'I've got you now, Dirk. You're quite safe. I am going to pull you out.' The boy was blubbering quietly. 'Dirk, listen to me. I need you to help me. Do you understand?' He felt the small hand squeeze his. 'Try to get your other hand free. I will hold you so you won't slip any further down.'

Nothing seemed to happen for a moment and Dirk whispered, 'I can't do it.'

Conn thought about what to do next and said, 'Try to get your other arm close to your body and then slowly, very slowly, wiggle it up towards your head.'

A face appeared at the entrance to the pit and Dirk's father, Rolf, peered in. His voice was strained with worry as he called out, 'What's happening down there?'

'Move away, you're blocking the light,' Conn shouted, not caring that this was disrespectful to an elder. Rolf's head moved away and Conn could see that Dirk had managed to wriggle his second hand free. He took hold of it and pulled. Nothing happened except he himself sank a little lower into the corn. He wondered what to do now. 'Dirk, I'm going to turn you round onto your back. Cross your hands.' He held firmly onto Dirk's wrists. 'Now try to turn yourself over.' Dirk began to twist and struggle until slowly his body began to turn and he had his back to Conn and the entrance. 'Now see if you can reach the wall with your feet,' Conn ordered.

'I can feel it,' Dirk called out.

'When I pull your hands, you push with your feet,' Conn said firmly. Slowly, like a stopper coming out of a bottle, the boy began to move towards Conn.

'Take in the rope about one pace,' Conn shouted from the pit. He felt the harness tighten and his body was hauled backwards.

'We'll do that again, Dirk,' Conn said encouragingly and they repeated the manoeuvre. Conn again called for the people above to pull on the rope. Once more he felt his body hauled backwards.

Little by little they crept backwards until the two of them were lying side by side, Dirk on his back and Conn on his stomach, under the entrance. Dirk was crying quietly now. A rope was lowered and Conn tied it under the boy's arms. He told the people above to pull gently and Dirk disappeared up through the hole. Immediately he felt the harness pull on him and he was quickly hauled up into the fresh air.

By now, more people had gathered and willing hands pulled him to his feet. Dug was there, blubbering like his brother, and Silda had her arms protectively round both her sons. As she and Morwen took the twins home, Rolf came over and clapped his hand on Conn's shoulder. 'Well done, boy, and thank you.' Conn could see tears in Rolf's eyes though he was trying hard to hold them back. 'Let's get this pit sealed up again.' Conn and he moved the slab of stone back over the entrance and pushed bits of clay and dung into the cracks, working in companionable silence. When they had finished Rolf said to Conn, 'Go and clean yourself up. Then we would all be very pleased if you could come and have some food with us.'

That evening the whole family looked on Conn as a hero. No one spoke about the incident in the pit, but Conn noticed that both Dirk and Dug squirmed uncomfortably on the floor so he guessed that Rolf had taken a strap to them. Conn sat next to Morwen during supper and he glowed with pleasure when she gently squeezed his hand.

Chapter 4
PLANNING

Publius Anicius Maximus was in rank third in command of the Second Legion after Vespasian and his brother Titus. He had joined the Augusta at Strasbourg during the German campaign in Caligula's second year as Emperor. Aged 50, he was the oldest of the legion's officers. His official title was *Praefectus Castrorum* or Prefect of the Camp, and his responsibilities were great. As Prefect he was responsible for the positioning of every legionary camp, direction of the entrenchments and inspection of the huts or tents. He had to make sure there was sufficient water supply to the camp, that there were adequate provisions and that the sick and wounded were properly looked after. As Prefect he was also in command of the specialist units like the artillery and carpenters every campaigning legion needed. One of his most important responsibilities was surveying and road building. In 4 years with the legion, Maximus had built hundreds of miles of new road, and had distinguished himself as an officer of great skill and imagination. Most important of all, he had the complete trust of Vespasian.

It was just after dawn and Maximus was prowling around the headquarters tent checking that everything was in order. This modest building was joined to the General's tent by a wooden partition. In truth both were more huts than tents, but Vespasian always called wherever he slept a tent while he was on campaign. Maximus knew exactly where everything was and where everything should be in the headquarters building because he had designed them himself. He unclipped a large wooden tabletop from a bracket securing it to the wall and carefully positioned this on a pair of wooden trestles, which had been neatly stacked in one corner. Then, with equal care, he placed three stools around the table. He then went to a wooden chest and collected three waxed boards with styluses and laid them on the table. Finally, with the same precision that dictated all his actions, he lifted out a long rolled parchment and placed it between the waxed tablets on the table. He heard a noise behind him and turning round saw a young man he did not recognise.

'Who are you?' Maximus asked sharply.

'Tribune Julius Graecinus of the Second Cohort, Sir.' This was followed by a parade-ground salute.

'What are you doing in the General's tent?'

'The Commander told me to report at first light, Sir, and the guard let me in.'

Maximus stormed to the entrance of the hut and found a soldier standing at ease. 'Do you let any unknown person who asks into the General's tent? How do you know this is not a Celt in disguise? How do you know the General is not lying in a pool of blood with his throat slit?'

The soldier snapped to attention and gazed impassively into the middle distance. 'The Tribune brought dispatches from Rome last night, Sir. The General told him to report this morning, Sir. He was not unknown to me, Sir.'

Maximus grunted. The guard knew that this was the closest he would get to an apology from the Prefect and inwardly smiled to himself, careful to make sure the smile did not show on his face. Maximus made his way back into the hut realising he had probably overreacted. Of all his responsibilities, protecting the General was one of the most difficult as Vespasian was always wandering off by himself leaving his bodyguards behind. But he nodded to himself; the guard should never have let the young tribune in without consulting him first.

As Maximus returned, Vespasian and Titus came in from their sleeping quarters. Vespasian nodded to Julius while Maximus drew up another stool. Vespasian sat down, and the others followed his lead.

'Greetings, Maximus. I hear you are in good voice.' Maximus looked down at the table while the two brothers smiled. 'I have heard from Rome. We have received orders to destroy the Durotriges and the Dumnonii. Our campaign will start as soon as the weather in this miserable place improves which will probably be around the middle of April. It may still be raining, but at least it should be warm rain. There is much to be done in the next three and a half months and planning must start now.' Vespasian unrolled the parchment on the table, holding down the two ends with the wine goblets, now empty, that he and Titus had brought in. 'Is this the best map we have?' he asked.

'Yes, Sir,' Maximus replied. 'I am filling in some of the details we have discovered from our last campaign and I have surveyors detailing the island of Vectis at the moment, but westwards we only have a coastal outline, and I am not very confident about that.'

Vespasian spread his hand over the map. 'From here at Chichester,' his hand moved to the left, 'to here where the land ends must be nearly 200 miles. We have three campaigning seasons to complete the job. Can it be done, Maximus?'

Maximus stood up and moved around the table. His bad temper forgotten, he frowned as he concentrated on the map. In his mind he saw the roads, legionary forts and marching camps that would be necessary. Vespasian did not try to hurry him, as he believed that his Prefect was the best engineer in the Roman army and his estimates now would dictate the planning of the whole campaign. Maximus looked up from the table. 'Yes, it can be done,' he declared.

Vespasian sighed with relief, but Titus stood up and turned to Maximus, shaking his head in exasperation. 'I know you're good, Maxim, but how can you possibly say that? You don't know what sort of resistance we might meet from the natives, or what problems with supplies we might have.'

Vespasian put his hand on his brother's shoulder to silence him. 'As always, Titus, Maximus will have already taken these things into account before he answered. He will have estimated how many supply ships might sink and he knows how long on average it takes to defeat one of the enemy's hillforts. He knows how many miles of new road he can lay each month. That is his job. Our job is to do the fighting.' He turned to Maximus. 'What standard of road have you estimated for, my friend?'

Maximus looked at the General. 'I have assumed roads of the second standard. These will last for 10 years rather than for 100. My men can lay 30 miles of this standard of road every 2 to 3 weeks. It will take on average 3 days to defeat a hillfort, less if the tribes can be persuaded to surrender before an attack. We will need three legionary fortresses here, here and here,' he said, pointing at the map. 'The first two will only need to house half the legion because half the soldiers and half the auxiliaries will be occupying captured hillforts. The one in this area,' he pointed towards the western end of the map, 'will have to be large enough to accommodate the whole legion. Furthermore we will need at least three supply harbours along the coast.'

Titus sat down again, humbled by Maximus's expertise. 'I am sorry I questioned your ability, Max. Thank the gods all I need to do is fight.'

Vespasian picked up one of the wax tablets and a stylus and turned to Maximus. 'What must we do immediately and how do we fill the next months?'

Maximus picked up another tablet. As he spoke he jotted down notes. 'Before April we must have decided on the site of our next legionary fortress and the first two supply harbours. These will determine the lines of our major roads. We must have an idea of the strength of the enemy in this area.' His hand lay flat on the map to the north-west of the island of Vectis. 'I shall, myself, choose the site for our first legionary camp and my team of surveyors will map the area and report on the strength of the enemy. We will need at least three centuries to protect us. I will have to use the navy to find our harbours. Rufius is the senior of my naval captains. He will take a small galley down the coast with one of my surveyors. He will have to put ashore in several places to find where the water is deep enough for our supply ships to run up onto the beach and to discover sources of drinking water. He will probably need an interpreter who can speak the native language.'

Julius, who had been listening to everything in silence, now spoke. 'General'. The other three looked up. 'I can speak the Celtic language, Sir. I learned it from the Venitii while I was with the Fourth Legion in Brittany. I would like to volunteer to accompany Captain Rufius.'

It never took Vespasian long to arrive at a military decision and he already trusted this young man. He scribbled something on the wax tablet and laid it on the table. 'Excellent,' he exclaimed. 'I shall go over to Vectis to inspect the five cohorts there in their winter quarters. Tribune Graecinus, you report to Captain Rufius. Maximus will give the Captain his general orders and you have my authority to fill in the details for him.' He pressed into the wax with his signet ring and handed Julius the tablet. 'Maximus, get together the force you need. We will all meet back here 1 month from today.'

'What about me? What orders do you have for me?' asked Titus.

'You are in charge here in my absence. As for what you do,' Vespasian smiled at his brother, 'what do the legions always do in winter? You train.'

Chapter 5
EXPLORATION

Julius left the tent clutching his wax tablet in a whirl of excitement. He was still tired after his frantic dash across Gaul but could not believe his good fortune at being given his first independent command at the age of 22 and he had absolutely no idea what to do next. He had just made up his mind to walk the 3 miles to the harbour to try to find Captain Rufius when he heard someone calling him.

'Come here, Tribune.' He looked round to see the grizzled third-in-command Publius Maximus waving at him. Maximus had not spoken a word to him during the meeting in the tent and Julius was a little afraid of the stern veteran.

'What are you going to do now?' Maximus demanded. Julius explained his intention to go and meet Captain Rufius and to plan the expedition.

Maximus was quiet for a while, rubbing his hand over his stubbly cheek, deep in thought. 'Come along to my hut,' he suddenly said and turning on his heel strode off to the north of the camp. Julius followed apprehensively.

Maximus's hut was a simple wooden building. It was plain and ordinary on the outside and just as plain inside. Julius could see no sign of any luxuries, and it appeared to be exactly the same standard of accommodation as the foot soldiers were used to.

Maximus pushed a wooden box towards Julius and gestured him to sit. He walked up and down for a while.

Julius recognised now that this was the Prefect's own peculiar method for collecting his thoughts and he remained silent. Maximus then spoke. 'Your expedition may seem to you to be a pleasant little boating trip, a good way to escape military duties, but the whole success of this summer's campaign may well depend on how well you carry out your orders.'

Julius started to speak, but Maximus waved him quiet. 'The General has given you command of this little expedition, but I will now tell you what I need from you. During the summer months the Augusta will march west. My engineers will build a legionary fortress and many miles of new roads and the soldiers will fight and defeat any enemy they come across. The General will want to move fast; he always does, and it will be my responsibility to keep him supplied. To achieve this I will have to find a series of safe havens, probably about 20 miles apart, where our ships can come close to the shore. We will build wharves and warehouses and some basic defences against raids from the neighbouring tribes. Your job is to find the sites for these bases; sites that have deep enough water so our ships can run onto the beaches at the top of the tide, but with easy access for us to move inland.'

Maximus moved over to the corner of the hut and selected a long roll of parchment. He stretched it out on the table and invited Julius over. He pointed to the map. 'This is Chichester where we are camped. Captain Rufius will sail up this coastline passed Vectis here, and together you will select three or four appropriate sites,' his hand moved over the map, 'here, here and here.' He took a stick of charcoal from his tunic pocket and marked three small black crosses on the map. 'No-one really knows what the coastline looks like to the west of here, so I will send one of my best young surveyors with you. I think Alexis will be the most suitable. He's a young Greek freedman and very experienced. He will bring back detailed plans of every bit of land you see. Do you understand what is required?'

Julius nodded and Maximus rolled up the parchment and handed it to him. 'Rufius is a good man and a fine sailor, but you have the General's authority so you must command. You will need to consider how many men you are going to take with you. When are you leaving? How long do you expect to be away? How much in the way of supplies will you need?' Maximus rattled off the questions. Julius admitted that he did not know any of the answers. Maximus sat down next to him and picking up a wax tablet began to jot down what was necessary. It took nearly half an hour for Julius to begin to understand the complexity of his command. By the time they had finished Julius and Maximus had decided that they should take enough supplies for 15 days and ten soldiers as well as Alexis.

'I will give orders to Lucius Vitellius as centurion to aid you. Rufius will look after the crew; that is not your worry. I will send him his instructions immediately. I suggest you go down to see him this afternoon.' With that Julius was dismissed.

Julius walked the 3 miles from the camp to the harbour after his midday meal and, arriving at the main thoroughfare, asked where he might find Captain Rufius. He was directed to a ship tied up at the furthest wharf. He was nervous about the meeting and wondered how he was going to impose his authority on someone who so far outranked him. Clutching the wax tablet with Vespasian's signet mark on it he stopped at the gang-plank.

The galley was much smaller than most of the supply ships in the harbour. It had 12 oars on each side and looked sleek and fast. The mast was stepped roughly at the mid-point of the hull and had a red and white striped sail furled at the yardarm. There was a long bowsprit sticking out at the front, which Julius knew could be used for additional sail, and two steerage oars, one either side of the stern post, joined together over the decking by a strong wooden batten. Two crewmen in the bows were coiling rope. From under a small awning in the stern emerged one of the biggest men Julius had ever seen. The man looked up and saw Julius standing on the quay.

'Hullo, Tribune!' he bellowed. 'Come on board.' Julius scrambled over the thwart of the galley and made his way aft to the large man. He held out his hand and Julius found it engulfed in a mighty paw. 'Welcome on board the *Astra*. I am Rufius, Captain of this fine ship.'

To his surprise Julius found he was no longer nervous of Rufius. The warm welcome, the twinkle in his eye and the general atmosphere of calm on the boat all helped to put him at his ease. He disengaged his hand from Rufius's grasp and started to pull out Vespasian's authorisation from his pocket. The Captain stopped him. 'Tribune, I know you are in command of this expedition. I have had my orders from Maximus and have no problem with that. You will direct where we are to travel, and will order the soldiers and do whatever you have to on land. However, on board, I give the orders.' Julius hastened to make it clear that he knew almost nothing about sailing, so that was fine by him. What had seemed like a potential problem evaporated under Rufius's good nature.

The two men sat down and started talking about food, weapons and tenting. Julius handed the Captain the outline of the plan that had been agreed with Maximus and Rufius studied it.

'Maximus is a fine soldier,' he said, 'one of the best; but he does not understand the sea. Sailing in the winter months is a tricky business. I reckon we have about 100 miles to travel and that is a long journey in these waters at this time of year. The *Astra* is sturdy and fast, but there is no way that I would want to be at sea in a ship of this size if there's a storm. We will have a full complement of 24 slaves to man the oars, but only 7 crewmen to manage the ship. I would like to wait for an east wind and a period of fair weather. We will try to find a secure anchorage each night and never sail too far from the shore in case the wind gets up.' He pointed to a small piece of cloth hanging from one of the shrouds which supported the mast. 'At present we have a wind from the west, and this misty rain. I expect the wind to change in a couple of days with the weather set fair. We would be much better to wait till then. Your basic plan looks sound though — 15 days at the outside should be plenty for this trip.'

Julius looked disappointed that they were not setting off immediately, but realised that Rufius knew what he was talking about.

'I'll get the soldiers and the food and tents organised,' he agreed, 'and meet you back here the day after tomorrow at first light.'

Sure enough, 2 days later Julius was relaxing on a heavy cushion in the stern of the Roman galley as it sailed slowly westwards down the line of the coast. From the sea, the low shore looked flat and featureless in the winter sunlight and the rhythmic beat of the oars threatened to send him to sleep. That was not what was expected of the commander of a Roman force even if the force was only ten strong and in no immediate danger. Julius shook himself awake and focused his eyes once more, looking for the gap in the coast that would enable him to fulfil the first part of his mission.

Julius looked at the small band of soldiers he now commanded. They were playing dice in the well of the ship and seemed happy enough. He had met Vitellius for the first time that morning. The centurion, he thought, lacked imagination, but would probably be dependable in a crisis. He was not joining in the soldiers' game, but they chatted to him in a relaxed but respectful way, which suggested that he should have little difficulty enforcing his orders. The morning was sunny and calm, as Rufius had predicted. On the Captain's command the rowers had taken them out of Chichester harbour shortly after dawn. Rufius had then swung the bows to the west and ordered the sail ties to be released. The slaves had pulled in their oars and all that morning the galley had drifted along through the narrows separating the mainland from the island of Vectis. Earlier they had passed one possible landing spot, a river mouth that could have provided a safe anchorage, but Julius reckoned it was still too close to Chichester to serve what Maximus required. In the afternoon the wind dropped altogether and Rufius ordered the slaves to start rowing again. All the time the young Greek, Alexis, had been sketching the shoreline. To Julius this looked remarkably featureless with low stunted trees and little sign of life, but Alexis' drawing on the papyrus brought it all to life, though the scribbled numbers and symbols on the top of the paper were meaningless to Julius.

'See there?' Julius pointed. 'There's a river mouth. We should go in and take a look.' Rufius gave the order to the steersman who swung over the heavy steering oars and the bows of the galley pointed at the narrow gap that Julius had indicated. As they drew closer to the shore the current against them grew stronger. The overseer urged the rowers to greater effort. Soon they were making almost no progress and it was all Rufius and the steersman working together could do to hold the galley's course.

After five static minutes Rufius gave the order to stop rowing. As the *Astra* slowly drifted sternwards he ordered a bucket to be lowered over the side. It was brought to him full of water and he dipped in his hands, took some water into his mouth and spat it out again. 'That's salt water coming out,' he said. 'What we have here is no river mouth, more of an inland sea. That's why the tide coming out is so strong. We will beach the *Astra* on the sand over there and tomorrow morning when the tide is with us we will have no difficulty entering the lagoon and exploring. This could be exactly the sort of place Maximus is looking for.'

Rufius ran the bows of the galley onto the sand and the crew-members stretched out a chain and anchor to secure her above the upper tide level. The soldiers soon had a fire going and tents erected on the beach. Julius ordered Vitellius to divide his small force into two watches to guard the camp. Rufius made certain that his crew and the rowers had sufficient food and shelter for the night. As the tide dropped the galley settled on the sandy beach and Julius decided to explore inland while there was still light. So far on the voyage he had not had much chance to talk to the young Greek surveyor, and this seemed a good opportunity to get to know him better.

'Alexis, you come with me. There's just enough time for us to see what there is over this sandbank, and to get an idea what we might find tomorrow.'

The two set off together and had not walked for many minutes inland before it became obvious that they were camped on a low peninsula of sand. On one side was the sea and on the other they could see the outline of a huge inland lake, like a lagoon, stretching for 4 or 5 miles inland.

'I think this tidal pool will provide Maximus with just the sort of harbour he needs for unloading supplies,' Alexis said. 'If it is acceptable to you, Tribune, I would like to explore it tomorrow and make some detailed drawings.' Julius agreed and excited by their find the two young men hurried back to camp.

Next morning they had to wait an hour after first light until the galley was comfortably floating on the rising tide. Rufius took his ship out to sea and pointed the bows at the gap Julius had spotted the day before. This time there was no problem as the ship was swept into the lagoon on the in-rushing tide, passing many small islands and sandy inlets. All morning they paddled the boat slowly round the eastern edge of the lagoon, which Alexis had marked on his chart as *Great Lagoon*. He sketched and scribbled on his scroll continuously as a sailor in the bows shouted the depth on the lead line. Every hour the leadman was changed as Alexis continued with his charting and plotting.

Around midday Rufius decided that his rowers needed a rest. He ran the bows of the galley onto a gravelly beach, which was protected on both sides by tidal inlets. Rufius and Julius decided that although still early this would be a secure place to spend the night and they would be able to float the *Astra* off the beach by the middle of next morning. One of the soldiers had spotted some native huts close to the shore and Vitellius asked permission to investigate. He returned well before supper to report to Julius that the locals were no threat.

The following day they continued their voyage of exploration. To the west they discovered the mouths of two rivers that emptied into the Great Lagoon. They rowed up the wider of these past colonies of seabirds and a barren shoreline of reeds and mudflats. Three miles from the river's mouth Julius reckoned he had found another place that would make a good landing spot. He asked Alexis to mark it on his map and to call it Morionium, after the village where his father was born. The river at Morionium was just broad enough for the galley to turn round and as the wind was beginning to freshen Rufius decided again for an early finish to the day's voyage. They pulled into the bank and tied up to some willow trees. That night a storm blew up.

For 3 days the storm raged. The ship was well protected by the banks of the river and they were in no danger, but it was wet and miserable for all of them huddled in the bottom of the boat with canvas tentage keeping off the worst of the rain. During the afternoon of the third day it stopped raining, but Rufius told Julius that they would not be able to move on until morning because of the level of the tide.

Again Julius decided he would like to do some exploring with Alexis. This time he took one of the soldiers with him for protection. Half a mile further up the river they came to a place where it was narrow and shallow enough to walk across. On the far bank were three small huts with fishing nets spread over the roofs. Julius decided this was as good a time as any to test out his language skills. The three of them waded across the river and approached the largest of the huts.

'Hello,' shouted Julius. The soldier, under strict orders from Vitellius, had already drawn his sword and they waited. An old man poked his head out of the doorway and, trying to remember the Celtic language he had learned in Gaul, Julius greeted him. He was met with a blank stare and silence. Again he tried his greeting and a second head appeared out of the gloom of the hut. A small and very dirty girl emerged slowly and spoke. Julius was delighted and relieved that the sentences spoken by this child were sufficiently similar to the language of the Venitii people in Gaul for him to understand most of what she said. The girl told him that the old man was her grandfather. She said he was deaf and stupid and her parents were away. Julius questioned further and the girl said she was a Durotriges, but that the three families –the girl indicated the other huts – lived away from the rest of the tribe. They were fishermen and the river, which she called the Isca Frome, had plenty of fish in it. He could not get any more information from her, but pleased with what he had learned Julius gave her a large hunk of the bread he was carrying. She glanced at the old man and, seeing he hadn't noticed the gift, she hid it in her shirt. The Romans turned, aware of eyes watching them as they waded back across the river.

Next morning, with the tide still 2 hours away from full, they made ready to sail. As the tide changed they were swept effortlessly out of the lagoon.

Chapter 6
SPIES

The storm had blown itself out and the morning was clear, crisp and cold. The *Astra* slowly sailed westwards driven by the regular beat of the oars. Rufius steered them on a path less than half a league from where the waves broke on the shore. They passed jutting headlands and shimmering white chalk cliffs. One break in the cliffs led to a small circular bay, which looked like a possible harbour, but Rufius pointed out that inland there was insufficient room for all the buildings necessary for a supply depot. Alexis nodded his agreement. They rowed on.

Throughout the journey Alexis had busied himself with writing and drawing. Julius, who had come to like the young Greek on their two trips inland, chatted with him. He asked him how it happened that he was working as a surveyor in the Roman army. Alexis continued to sketch the cliff line. Slowly at first, and then with growing confidence, he began to talk. He explained that his parents had been household slaves to the family of a rich senator in Rome. His father had kept the accounts and had been greatly trusted. As a boy Alexis was allowed to run around the servants' quarters and the garden. One day the senator had found him drawing in a corner of the garden and had recognised that he had talent. In a generous gesture he allowed the young boy to join his own children in lessons with a tutor. It soon became obvious that Alexis had inherited his father's skill with numbers and he excelled in maths. His parents had been granted their freedom when he was 15, but both had continued to work for the senator. Alexis was sent to army school to learn surveying. One year later while he was at the school, Alexis was orphaned and found himself without a patron. The senator was one of those who opposed the Emperor Caligula's reign of terror. Suspicion had fallen on him and during the night the Emperor's guards had come to the house and put to death everyone they found.

Alexis stopped talking for several minutes and gazed at the landscape with added concentration. Julius tactfully did not say anything, giving his new friend time to compose himself. 'I did well in the school and found favour with my instructors,' he continued. 'Four years ago I was sent to Germany to join the Second Legion and the legion is now my family.'

Julius felt great warmth towards his companion and realised that the two of them could become close friends. He studied Alexis's drawings and complimented him on his skill. He then told him his own, far more conventional history. As the two young men talked, the chalk cliffs of the shoreline gradually changed, giving way to a beach, first pebbles and then a long wide expanse of sand. A small river flowed out into the bay, and it was to here that Rufius steered the *Astra*. The order was given to stop rowing and the ship glided silently forward until the keel grated on the yellow beach.

'What now?' Julius wondered. He had not yet thought through what they were going to do next. He looked over towards Rufius. The Captain was issuing a string of orders to the seamen who were securing the boat to the shore. Remembering their first friendly conversation at the harbour near Chichester, Julius did not think his authority would be compromised if he discussed options with his companions. He asked Rufius, Alexis and the centurion Vitellius to join him on the beach.

'What do you recommend as a plan of action, Captain Rufius?' he asked.

Rufius looked round thoughtfully. 'The tide is at its lowest. If we camp here for the night, my sailors can gradually ease the ship up the beach as the water comes in to make it secure. I suggest that is as far west as we need to go this trip. The bay looks like an excellent landing spot if we can find somewhere with deep water close to the shore.' He turned and pointed to the wall of dark rock that seemed to block their progress further westwards. 'Tomorrow I would like to take my ship along the coast of that island, just to see what's at the end there. From past experience, Maximus always wants to know what is round the next corner. This river here looks worth exploring and, if I can find a solid anchorage in it, here should be our most westerly point for this year's campaign. With the prevailing wind blowing from the south-west, it shouldn't be more than two full days sailing back to Chichester. As long as we don't have prolonged storms I think we can afford a little time here to explore inland.'

Julius was grateful to the Captain for such a clear suggestion of a way forward. He turned to Vitellius. 'What do you think, centurion?'

Vitellius was not used to being asked his opinion; usually it was just a matter of carrying out orders. He thought for a moment. 'I have seen several natives on the cliff top as we have been passing along, but nothing that soldiers of the Second can't look after. If we set up camp here, my men can protect the boat.' His stolid confidence was reassuring to Julius.

Julius looked at Alexis. 'That's settled then, you and I will explore inland. It's too late to set off now. We'll start tomorrow early and take enough food with us for the day. You also need to bring your drawing kit. Captain, when your ship is afloat you do your exploring and find our landing site. Centurion, you and your men pitch the tents here. Your job is to guard both ship and camp.'

Vitellius looked worried. 'Don't you want me to come with you, Tribune?' he asked. 'Praefectus told me to keep you safe.'

Julius laughed. 'No thank you, Vitellius.' The last thing he and Alexis wanted was an old foot plodder to nanny them. 'I don't expect anything nasty to happen to us here. We should be back by nightfall. Captain, if we don't turn up by mid- morning on the day after, you are to sail back to Chichester without us,' he said with bravado.

Early next day the two young men set off, delighted with the freedom this exploration gave them. They noticed a small collection of huts on the far bank near the mouth of the river a good distance away from them. A dog barked at them across the water, but they saw no one about. Almost immediately the river widened into a pool with golden reeds marking the shore-line. Alexis pointed out a heron fishing in the shallows, which flapped lazily away as they approached. The water was crowded with feeding ducks and geese. They continued up the river through clumps of willow along a rough track. Occasionally the path led them through shallows and they startled the wild fowl that were splashing on the edge of the water. After nearly 2 miles, where the river began to narrow, the path crossed the water by a ford and Julius and Alexis decided to follow it over. Once on the far bank they started to climb the hill in front of them.

Three hours after they had left the *Astra* Julius called a halt. The friends sat down on the grass and Julius pulled out some bread and cheese from his pack. Alexis emptied his pack also and gazing back the way that they had come he started to sketch as they ate. 'Look, there is the *Astra*.' He pointed with his stick of charcoal. 'With her oars out she looks like a beetle crawling along the line of the cliffs. From here I think the island looks to be the shape of a swan's beak, so I will call it The Beak. He scribbled the name onto his map and looked up again pointing excitedly to Julius. 'See how the coastline sweeps to the right of the island into another great bay. Actually it isn't an island at all. Look. It's connected to the land by that long pebble bank stretching as far as you can see.' With four or five skilled strokes of charcoal the outline of the coast was captured on paper. Julius lay back on the grass admiring his friend's talent. Above him a buzzard mewed to a distant mate as it gracefully spiralled in the thermals high above the ridge. He rolled onto his stomach and noticed two oxen emerging from the wood to their left. Driving the small brown hairy oxen was a scrawny young boy wearing a kilt of rough cloth, leather sandals and a sheepskin jacket. The boy looked suspiciously at the two strangers.

'Hello,' said Julius. He unbuckled his sword, laid it on the grass and advanced on the boy with his hands held sideways to show he was unarmed. The boy put his hand into a pouch at his belt and pulled out a round stone and threatened Julius with it.

'What's your name, boy?' Without waiting for a reply Julius continued, 'Come and share our food.'

Julius and Alexis sat down on the grass again and Alexis held out the bread and cheese. The boy drove a stake into the ground to secure the oxen. Warily coming towards Alexis he snatched the offered food.

'My name is Conn,' he said eventually, and took a huge bite out of the cheese.

While Alexis kept the hungry boy supplied with more of their breakfast, Julius continued to ply him with questions. Though still cautious, Conn's attitude began to thaw as he ate and he explained that he had come here to plough. He pointed out to them his simple *ard* plough behind the oxen, which was nothing more than an angled beam of wood with a metal spike fastened to the end. Eventually he asked if they would like to see the field where he had to work and when Julius said they would, he led them round the corner and pointed out three narrow ploughed terraces on the hillside. Conn explained that as numbers in their community had grown so they had had to plough more and more land on the side of the hills furthest away from their houses. 'This is terrible soil,' he said. 'After I have ripped up the grass with the *ard* I have to bash the turfs with my *mattock* to break them down. This year there was too much bad grass to plant corn in the dying of the year and I have had to plough it three times to remove the weeds.' Julius did not know much about farming, but bending down he saw that despite Conn's triple effort with the plough there was still quite a lot of couch grass in the tilled earth. Conn added, 'We will plant these fields with beans next year.'

The three young men sat down on the grassy bank at the edge of the field. Alexis started to sketch and Julius got out a flask of wine and two cups. Conn was still suspicious of the two strangers and began to ask questions. 'What's he doing and why doesn't he speak?' Julius explained that Alexis was an artist and he didn't know the Celtic language so could not join the conversation. 'Where are you from, and what are you doing here?' Conn continued.

Julius thought quickly and decided it was unlikely that the boy had heard of Rome. It was time for some deception.

'We're merchants from Gaul,' he said. 'We've come to see if there are opportunities here for trading.'

'Is that your ship in the bay?' Conn asked, pointing to the tiny shape of the *Astra*. 'I noticed it earlier. What is it you are selling?'

'We're traders in pottery,' Julius replied. He handed his drinking bowl to the boy who studied it closely.

'We have plenty of pottery of our own,' Conn said, 'but ours is much heavier and coloured black. I like the markings on this, but I don't think anyone in our tribe will

44

want to buy from you.'

Julius wanted further information and thought that a small present might soften the boy. 'You can keep it if you want. We have a whole shipful down there.'

Conn accepted the present and put it inside his shirt. 'I think Bannoc has a red cup just like this in his house.' With a little prompting from Julius, Conn went on to explain that Bannoc was the Chieftain of Mai-dun. 'He's the best fighter of all the tribes. All the other chieftains are frightened of him.' Conn was in full flow now. 'No-one has dared to attack Mai-dun for hundreds of years because our fort is too strong, and when we raid Bannoc is always winning victories. I hate farming and want to join our fighters. Bannoc says I have to wait until I'm 15 before I can train as a slinger.' Shyly he drew out a weapon from his pouch. It consisted of two rough woollen straps joined together by a broad strip of leather. 'I've been practising though. Can I show you?' His hand dived into his pouch again and drew out one of the smooth pebble stones that he had threatened Julius with earlier. 'We call these chesils and collect them from the beach down there.' He fitted the pebble in the leather strip, twirled the sling three times round his head and released one end. The stone flew across the field and smacked into the trunk of an oak tree 50 paces away. Conn grinned, pleased with his accurate aim.

Julius had seen slingers in the Roman army, but even so he was impressed by Conn's skill. One more question needed to be asked. 'Where is your settlement?'

'We can leave the oxen where they are,' Conn said in reply, beckoning them to follow. He ran up to the crest of the hill and pointed north. 'Mai-dun, that's my home.' Julius and Alexis could see the outline of a vast hillfort about 3 or 4 miles away. They could recognise three distinct rings of ramparts and trenches with a climb of well over a hundred feet to the top. Inside the final palisade they could see clearly columns of smoke from over 200 fires drifting through the

45

thatch of the crowded houses. 'Mai-dun means Great Hill,' Conn said proudly.

Julius knew he was now in possession of important military information. He felt uncomfortable at the thought he was spying and taking advantage of Conn's innocence, but he knew he must get a record of everything they had seen back to Maximus. He turned to Alexis and spoke to him in Latin. 'We must get this fortress marked on the map. You move along the ridge a couple of hundred paces till you are out of sight, while I talk to Conn here and see what more I can dig out of him. Draw the defences with as much detail as you can and make sure you have it accurately positioned in relation to our camp on the beach. I will meet you at the place where we crossed the river in a couple of hours.' Alexis waved to Conn and moved off.

Julius restarted the conversation by admiring the hillfort. 'Mai-dun looks very beautiful and so big. How many are there in your community, Conn?'

'Hundreds,' Conn answered waving his hand vaguely. And despite Julius's request for a better estimate, particularly of the number of fighting men, it became obvious that the boy wasn't going to give any more accurate figures. Conn stared into Julius's face for some minutes in silence, then sat down on the turf. *What is happening now?* Julius thought. He squatted down next to the boy, uncertain what to do next. He knew he should question Conn more rigorously to find out details of Mai-dun's defences. Maximus would expect that. But Conn, though sitting upright, seemed to have gone into a kind of trance.

'How many slingers in Mai-dun?' Julius tried again.

After a long pause Conn started to speak but his earlier suspicions had returned. 'Why are you asking me these things? Why do you need to know about the number of slingers in Mai-dun if you are selling pots? I thought you were a friend, but now I think you're just a dirty spy.'

Julius protested half-heartedly, but his words made no

impression on the boy. He was wondering how he could suitably end the meeting when Conn resolved this for him by spitting in his face and hurling a clod of earth at him. Humiliated, Julius decided that his best course of action was to retreat. He took one more look at Mai-dun, turned and strode off down the hill past the oxen, retrieving his sword on the way.

Two hours later Julius and Alexis met up at the river crossing. Alexis questioned his friend as to what he had found out, but Julius, reluctant to admit his embarrassment, muttered that Conn had not told him much more. The two decided to return to the beach by the opposite bank of the river. There they found a well-worn footpath and plenty of signs of habitation. As they drew close to the beach they came to the small village they had spotted on their outward journey. This time they were not so lucky and were quickly noticed. A shout went up and a group of six or seven men and women spilled out of the huts and started advancing towards them brandishing sticks. Julius drew his sword and Alexis picked a stout pole from the hedge. 'Let's try to slip round to the right and work our way to that building near the beach,' Julius said, pointing. 'From there we should be able to make a quick dash to the river and swim across. We should have gone back the way we came. I'm sorry to have put you in danger. Most important, if we get to the water you must keep your drawings dry.' Alexis gave him a quick smile and they both began to edge away from the approaching crowd. One man, who was bigger than the rest, saw what they were trying to do and moved to cut them off. Julius realised that they would have to fight their way out and quickly the two rushed at the big Celt, taking him by surprise. The man tumbled over with Alexis on top of him. The rest of the villagers let out a howl and ran towards the struggling figures.

They would certainly have overpowered the two young men within a few minutes, but a loud shout from the river stopped them in their tracks. Vitellius and four soldiers were crashing across the shallow water waving swords and spears. They arrived at the tangle of figures on the ground and Vitellius, standing with his foot on the hairy Celt's chest, helped Alexis to his feet. He looked at Julius and pressed his sword against the man's throat. 'Shall I finish him off?' Julius shook his head. 'I thought you said nothing nasty could happen to you here, Sir,' Vitellius said, smiling. 'I didn't like the look of this lot, so we were on watch for your return. Just as well if you ask me.' He sheathed his sword, ignoring the man still at his feet on the ground, who lay still long after the Romans had gone. The seven of them waded back across the river, now shallow at the turn of the tide, and made their way back to where the others were waiting.

The soldiers had just started to break camp and Julius found the *Astra* afloat and Captain Rufius ready to sail. However, the hours of daylight in winter were short and after discussion it was agreed that they should spend a further night on the beach. Rufius reported to Julius that he had found an ideal landing area further up the river that could be reached at high tide. He agreed to give the details to Alexis on the journey back so he could add this to his map. The two men could think of nothing further that needed to be done on this mission and Rufius calculated that with a south-westerly wind they could easily make it back to the sandbank camp next day. From there it should only be one further day back to the legionary headquarters at Chichester.

Chapter 7
WINTER SOLSTICE

Conn returned to Mai-dun after his meeting with Julius, keeping the small drinking bowl hidden. As soon as he entered his hut Kareth's gimlet eyes spotted the bulge in his shirt and she demanded, 'What have you got there?' Conn knew that if she saw the bowl he would have to give it up and he turned away from her saying nothing. He desperately wanted to keep it as he had so few treasures in the world. Kareth called to her husband who was outside. 'Gwillam, the boy has stolen something and won't show me what it is. Make him give it to me.'

The old man came into the hut unbuckling his leather belt. 'Come here, boy,' he said. Conn thought that in a fair fight he could have possibly got the better of the old man, but he knew it would not be a fair fight. Once before he had stood up to Gwillam, but for that impertinence he had been well thrashed by one of the Elders. In silence he handed the bowl to Kareth who cackled with pleasure. As Gwillam advanced towards him Conn put his arms up to protect his head. He felt the leather strap bite into his shoulder and gasped with pain. He knew what was coming, as he had been frequently thrashed, but this time he was determined not to cry out. He stood facing the old man. Again and again the belt cracked onto his arms and back, but Conn bit into his lip and maintained his silence. Gwillam quickly tired of his sport. It wasn't much fun if the victim wasn't squirming and crying on the floor. He threw his belt into the corner and told Kareth that Conn wasn't to have any food, before shuffling once more outside. Conn lay down on his mat. His shoulders and back ached from the belt, but the pain kept his mind sharp as he plotted his revenge. Before he went to sleep he saw Kareth hide the bowl among the roofing reeds and he swore that he would take it back soon.

The following morning was wet. The rain, driven by the wind, cut through the thin walls of the hut and dampness crept under the eaves of the thatch. Heavy cloud shrouded the whole valley. Conn gently flexed his shoulders and back where Gwillam's belt had cut his flesh. Kareth reluctantly told him that there was no point in taking the oxen out that day. She ordered him to fetch some water from the dew pond and shambled out to relieve herself. While she was away Conn found the little bowl where she had put it under the thatch of the roof. He smuggled it out of the hut and hid it in the woodpile near the doorway. He then picked up a wooden bucket and went off to collect water as he had been instructed. When he returned, Kareth thrust a bowl of porridge at him, which he ate in silence. As he scraped the bowl clean Conn's spirits began to lift. This might be a poor day for farming, but the bad weather gave him a free day to explore with his friend and it was with a light heart that he set off to find Huw. As he left the hut he slipped the little bowl inside his shirt.

Huw's family were just finishing tidying their hut, something that happened infrequently with Kareth and Gwillam. Conn proudly produced the bowl he had been given from under his shirt and it was passed round with many admiring comments. The small bowl was bright red in colour and had a hunting scene incised on the outside. It was obviously of far higher quality than the rough burnished black pots produced locally. Conn told them it had been a present from a stranger, and Rolf said that he thought it was from overseas, possibly from Gaul or Germany. He suggested that Conn took it to Maddoc, the Teacher, who was knowledgeable in all things. The two boys agreed that this was a good idea and ran up the main street through the rain to Maddoc's hut.

Maddoc had arrived at Mai-dun, escorted by a young companion, shortly after Bannoc, Rolf and the other leaders had taken over the community. As a young man he had trained with the Druids on the island of Mona and at Mai-dun he had quickly acquired a reputation for wise counsel. He was one of the few who could contradict the Chief without fear of his fierce temper. Behind his long grey hair and beard his eyes were surprisingly youthful. No one seemed to know much of his early history, or thought it respectful to ask. Since his young servant had died four years ago, the Teacher had lived by himself. Most of the settlers came to him at some time or other to tap his knowledge of healing, animal husbandry or what the future might hold. Maddoc was the spiritual leader of Mai-dun and those who sought his advice invariably left behind a chicken, some corn or ale, so he was never hungry or thirsty. Conn and Huw, along with the other children of the settlement, had all in their time learned from him about the wildlife around their home as well as having their various injuries tended to. All the boys took it in turns to fetch water and wood for him. This was considered an honour not an imposition. For the last 12 months Maddoc had taken a particular interest in Conn who had become a regular visitor to his home.

Maddoc was sitting on the floor of his hut chanting near to the blazing hearth when the two boys poked their heads around the doorpost. In his right hand he was holding a chain that was supporting a small metal dish from which a pungent smoke drifted up. Conn was uncertain whether

51

he was praying or singing to himself. Despite having frequently attended the old man throughout the summer he still had no idea what it was all about. The boys waited quietly in the doorway until Maddoc had finished and had laid the dish on the floor. They then came into the hut and sat down silently on the other side of the fire.

'Good morning, boys. How can I help you?' Maddoc asked quietly. Conn fished out his bowl and handed it over without a word. Maddoc turned it over in his hands, studying it carefully. His fingers traced out the incised design. 'The clay is much lighter in colour than ours.'

He ran his hand over the smooth texture. 'I believe the cup is Roman,' he said. 'The picture I think is of one of their goddesses and this type of clay work I have heard called Samian. It was made either for a wealthy Roman citizen or for an army officer. I believe it came originally from a country called Greece. How did you get this?' He stared hard at Conn. As usual, Conn felt that the old man could see right into his soul and he squirmed uncomfortably.

Conn did not know what a Roman was, but he told his story of seeing the boat at sea and meeting Julius and Alexis on the Ridgeway. He described Julius's clothes and the drawing that Alexis was making. He finished rather lamely by saying that he had been given the bowl as a present.

While travelling around Britain Maddoc had heard stories of earlier invasions, and recent visitors to Mai-dun had passed on rumours of fighting in the east. 'These men could be traders, or it might mean something more serious for us,' he said. 'I will have to think about it. Meanwhile you may keep your present.' Conn decided not to tell him about the information on Mai-dun he had shared with Julius. He asked Maddoc if he could leave the bowl with him for safe-keeping. It was not difficult for the wise man to realise the reason for this request and he quickly agreed. 'I will put it on this shelf and you can collect it whenever you want,' he said to the boy.

It had stopped raining and the clouds were starting to lift as the two friends made to leave the hut. 'Conn, I need your help with the bones,' Maddoc said. 'I think there is just about sufficient sun.' Conn led Maddoc round to the south side of his hut to an area he knew well. There was a small lean-to with a thatched roof. Conn knew that the whole roof could be detached in sunny weather. In the wet of that winter's day it was firmly attached and had kept the shelter dry from the rain. A pale shaft of sunlight shone through a gap in the wall. The floor was smooth, beaten earth. Stuck in the earth were 40 or 50 small pieces of animal bone making a strange pattern like an irregular spider's web. The first time Conn had helped Maddoc with the bones, the old man had explained to him what he was doing. 'Every day when the sun is shining I measure where the shadow falls by placing one of these markers in the ground. At the middle of the day when the shadow is at its furthest point I push the bone firmly into the ground to mark it. Any gaps show the days when there is no sun. In the summer when the days are long the shadow is shortest.' Maddoc pointed to a tight cluster of bones in the middle of the floor. At first Conn had been confused about what he was supposed to do, but after not very many days as helper he had grasped the idea behind the strange patterns. 'This is the way I can tell when the year is turning and the sun has started its long journey to come back to us,' Maddoc had explained. On this day he seemed more anxious than usual. 'Do you think there is enough sun to cast a shadow, Conn?'

Conn peered at the bones. 'There's a faint shadow, Teacher.'

'You must place this bone,' and he handed Conn a dried sheep's rib, 'exactly where the shadow finishes.' Conn pushed the bone into the beaten earth. 'How does it lie with the other tall bone?'

'Very close by, Teacher,' Conn answered. 'It's about a finger's width further from the outside wall. '

'That other tall bone is yesterday's mark,' the old man said. 'As the new marker you have just placed is closer to the centre it means we have passed the death of the year. It is now time for me to do what is necessary. Tomorrow I will celebrate the *mysteries* and I would like you to assist me. I also need a maid from our tribe that is unsullied. I think perhaps Alaynor would be a good choice this year.'

Conn was uncertain what unsullied meant, but if the stories he had heard from the other boys were correct it was unlikely that Alaynor was that. 'What about Morwen?' he asked.

Maddoc nodded. 'Ah yes, Morwen. Excellent.' He smiled at the boy. 'I shall ask Morwen.'

The next day Conn was striding along the bank of the *Isca Frome*. The weather had cleared and it was a crisp frosty winter's morning. He had been able to tell the old woman that he was to be busy all day working for the Teacher; she had grumbled, but there was nothing she could say to counter an order from one of the Elders. Maddoc's instructions had been quite clear. Conn was to collect a bag full of leaves from the evergreen shrub called myrtle, which grew on the north bank of the river near the oxen ford. Maddoc had shown a leaf to Conn and made him smell the distinctive bitter-sweet scent. 'You must not come back until you have found some more of it. On your way back you must also collect an armful of birch twigs from the wood near the standing stone.' It took him a short time to find the right shrub, and it was not one he had ever seen before. He carefully picked the green leaves and filled the leather bag he carried over his shoulder. Then, having collected as many dead birch sticks as he could carry, he set off to return the 3 miles to Mai-dun.

When he arrived back at Maddoc's hut he called out and

pushed his way past the hanging ox skin in the entrance. The fire was blazing and Maddoc was sitting in his usual place next to the hearth. Instead of the woollen cloak he always wore, he had on a fine red gown of woven material. It was the most beautiful piece of cloth Conn had ever seen. He signalled the boy to put some of the birch on the fire and as the flames reached higher the hut filled with a strong smell of the smoke. Behind Maddoc Conn could see someone working in the corner. As she came forward he recognised Morwen. She was wearing a long white dress tied at the waist with a green sash. Her fair hair had been combed out and lay long and golden down her back. Conn was stunned by her beauty and tried to catch her eye, but the girl was concentrating hard on the bowl she carried, which she offered to the Teacher. Conn squatted down by the fire and Maddoc, drinking deeply from the bowl, started chanting. Morwen signalled to Conn to hand over the bag with myrtle leaves. She sprinkled some of the leaves in the hearth where they spurted for a while, then caught fire. The leaves gave off a perfume-like scent, which Maddoc leaned forward and inhaled. The priest, for Conn realised that he was now more priest than teacher, continued with his chanting. Morwen moved slowly around the hut like a sleepwalker whose every movement was carefully controlled. Conn worried that she was unwell, but her eyes seemed to be lively enough. He saw her collect a chicken from the back of the hut and noticed that its legs were tied together with twine and its wings had been clipped. Morwen stroked its neck to calm it down and handed it to Maddoc. He picked up a small dagger that lay hidden by the hearth and swiftly and expertly cut its head off. He let the blood drain into the bowl and drank from it.

No longer chanting, Maddoc now spoke in a strong voice. 'Out of this death shall come rebirth. Out of the death of this year there shall be a renewal.' He continued to speak, but Conn could no longer understand what was said as it was in no language he had heard before. Eventually Maddoc fell silent and appeared to be in a trance. Morwen stood behind him and Conn squatted in silence. The boy had no idea how long the three of them remained in their positions, but eventually Maddoc sighed and opened his eyes. Morwen waved her hands at Conn for him to leave the hut and as he went out he saw that she was helping Maddoc up from the floor and leading him to a bed along the wall of the hut.

Conn had never been involved in any sort of religious ceremony before and he was shaken and confused by what he had witnessed. He tried to find Huw so that he could tell his friend everything that had happened, but one of the twins told him that the slingers had gone to the beach to collect chesils. He wandered around the settlement for a while and then decided to go back to the Teacher's hut and wait to be summoned. It seemed a long time before he heard Morwen calling him.

When Conn re-entered the hut Maddoc was sitting in his usual place, once again wearing his grey woollen surcoat. He looked wide-awake. Morwen too was in her everyday clothes and her hair was once more tied up. Maddoc invited both of them to sit down. 'Thank you for your help. Let me explain to you, Conn, what we have been doing this morning.' He stopped, thought awhile and started again. 'Every year, like all the druid priests who have trained at the Great Henge or on the island of Mona, I must celebrate the *mysteries* – once at the death of the old year and again at the summer turning of the year. Your help with the bones, Conn, tells me when this is. The birch twigs that you collected ward off any dangerous or evil spirits by filling the house with their smoke. The scent of the myrtle leaves helps me to think more clearly. Sometimes when I am in this state of half wakefulness I can see into the future. This is something like a dream, but, unlike a dream, I have learned to control when this is to happen. This year Morwen has been my helper. Many years ago I believe that some Druids used to sacrifice a maid at the ceremony of the summer mysteries, but that was before my time. Now we use a chicken.' He laughed and carried on. 'Morwen's main responsibility was to save me from having to get up and down all the time and to make sure I didn't fall into the fire.'

Conn was so relaxed by these gentle and humorous words that he thought he could risk a question. 'Did you see ...,' he hesitated, 'could you tell ... what is going to happen to us?'

Maddoc leaned forward with his elbows on his crossed knees and his beard resting on his folded hands. 'I did have a dream,' he said, 'but I do not yet understand what it means. There is a time of sorrow coming to our people. I saw a strong wind blowing across our land and some of our people it took up and dashed down to the ground, others it left alone.' He paused and his head slumped down. 'Thank you both for helping me today. You must leave now for I am tired.'

Outside the hut, as they walked home, Conn spoke nervously to Morwen, trying to put into words a feeling that had been troubling him. 'You know I have told you before how, sometimes, I have strange "seeings"... like dreams only I'm awake. I had one yesterday when I was up on the hill with that foreign man. It was horrible. I saw blood and crying and there was so much noise, I was really scared. Do you think the Teacher was talking about the same thing?'

On several occasions in the past Morwen had listened to Conn's stories of his visions. When these had left him feeling distressed she had been able to comfort him. Once again she put her arm round him and gave him a hug. 'Mai-dun is the best-defended hillfort anywhere. Whatever troubles are coming to the Durotriges, I am certain we will be safest here.' The feel of her body pressed against his side comforted Conn, but even this did not dispel his feeling of unease.

Chapter 8
STRATEGY

When he reached Chichester Julius learned that Vespasian, delayed by bad weather, was not yet back from his visit to the cohorts who were in winter quarters on Vectis. Julius decided to make his report to Maximus who was back in camp.

Next morning he presented himself at Maximus's hut. The guard announced him formally as Tribune Julius Graecinus and Maximus welcomed him inside. The hut looked just as stark as before, but Julius noticed that on the wall was a new map, drawn on a magnificent piece of vellum, now filled in with considerable detail including the discoveries he and Alexis had made during their voyage in the *Astra*. Maximus, looking pleased with himself, led Julius over to the map. Julius was proud to see that the village he had called Morionium was marked.

'Alexis brought his drawings and plans to me last night and we spent several hours putting them together on this map,' he said. 'You have done well, Tribune. The landing places you discovered, which Alexis called the Great Lagoon, will give us excellent bases for this year's campaign. The first place I have called Lagoon Harbour and for the landing site on the river,' he pointed across the water, 'I have used the name you gave, Morionium. Lagoon Harbour is only 5 miles from the spot I have chosen for our legionary headquarters on the river they call Stour.'

'*Isca Stour*.' Julius spoke with more confidence now.

'What is that?' asked Maximus.

'*Stour* means *powerful* in Celtic and *Isca* is the word they use for *river*. This river is called *Powerful Water* in their language. The other river by Morionium is *Isca Frome* which means *Fair Water*.'

'Well, this year's campaign is likely to be up the valley of the Powerful Water,' said Maximus. 'Your discovery and Alexis's drawings of Mai-dun will also be very useful, but we are unlikely to get there until next campaigning season. The Commander arrives back tomorrow. Expect to be called to a staff meeting.' With that Julius was dismissed and he made his way back to the hut he shared with the other young officers.

Vespasian did return from Vectis the next day, but it was 3 more days before Julius was summoned to a meeting of the General's staff. The headquarters hut was already crowded when Julius arrived just before midday. He recognised Gaius, one of the oldest tribunes, sitting alone on a raised platform against the far wall, and Vitellius, his protector on the voyage, who was talking to another centurion. Julius sat next to him and Vitellius introduced his companion as Centurion Carinus. Julius looking round and spotted Rufius leaning against the wall but did not know any of the other officers. Everyone stood as Titus and Maximus entered the room. Maximus fixed a map to the wall. Julius recognised this as the same map he had seen in the Prefect's hut, but there were now more arrows and lines marked on the mainland. Titus waved everyone to be seated and there was just a gentle murmuring as everyone awaited the arrival of the General.

Vespasian entered, wearing full military uniform, his scarlet cloak contrasting with everyone else's drab working clothes. There was absolute silence. Like an actor commanding the centre stage he looked around the room. Slowly he unbuckled his short sword and laid it on the table. Still in silence he walked to the centre of the room and stood with his legs apart. He looked every bit the commander and Julius felt a tingle of awe run through him. This was not the easy relaxed man he had met when first he came to the camp.

'I bring you greetings from your comrades in the Fifth and Sixth Cohorts in their winter quarters on Vectis.' Vespasian spoke quietly but his audience, aware they were about to hear what the future held for them, missed not a word. 'The Sixth Cohort has been involved in some light skirmishes with the local tribes, but our losses were small and all units are back in camp. I am told your training is going well and our legionaries are ready for action. This I can now promise you. The Emperor has entrusted to us, his Second Legion, the renowned Augusta, the task of conquering and controlling the whole south coast of this country. The enemy tribes are ferocious fighters and believe they are safe in their hillforts. When our legions appear they will retreat behind their defences, but we shall sweep them away, like a fierce wind sweeps away the leaves of autumn. The aim of our campaign this year will be to shock our enemies and to overawe them into believing resistance will be fatal for them. The Third and Fourth Cohorts commanded by my brother, Titus Flavius, will fight their way up the valley of this river Stour.' He went over to the map and traced with his finger the line of the assault.

'This campaign will start in around 4 weeks when the mornings begin to get lighter. For now the First and Second Cohorts will be in a supporting role if they are needed.' There was a murmur of disappointment at Vespasian's news from the centurions of the First Cohort, which was usually entrusted with any assault. He let the noise quieten and then went on.

'By autumn the legion will have captured and neutralised all these hillforts, built quarters for themselves and filled our granaries with native corn from the north.' Vespasian looked around the room. 'The first two cohorts supported by those from Vectis will be preparing our lines of attack for next year. Don't worry, there will be plenty of fighting for all of you too. The First and Second Cohorts will start by building our new legionary fort here, which I am calling *Lake Camp*. You can see it is right beside the River Stour. These troops will be commanded by the Prefect, Publius Maximus. He will give you your orders later. I am promoting Poenius Gaius Postumus to Senior Tribune in charge of the Fifth and Sixth Cohorts. These will be building the road system to advance our campaign. Marcus Carinus will become *Primus Pilus* in charge of the First Century.' Vitellius slapped his friend on the back and all around the hut there were nods of approval. Carinus was a much-respected soldier.

'The First and Second Cohorts will be responsible for our supply bases at Lagoon Harbour and Morionium.' Vespasian pointed these out on the map. 'Next year your men will lead our assault up this river Frome. Our spies have told us of a major hillfortress 25 miles up this valley. I can promise you there will be plenty of fighting. I leave the Praefectus and our new Senior Tribune to tell you more. I am honoured to be the commander of the Emperor's own legion.'

He turned to leave the room, but at the last moment turned back to them. 'Remember, we fight under the banner of Mars, the God of War. We are the fierce wind of autumn.'

Half an hour later the two brothers were sitting at ease in Vespasian's tent. 'A fierce wind of autumn; very poetic,' teased Titus, laughing.

Vespasian looked serious. 'I have to get everyone, including you Titus, to understand the need for speed. Our campaign must not get bogged down in long sieges.'

'You can depend on me, brother,' said Titus. 'My command will be a storm of efficiency.'

Maximus and Gaius Postumus entered the tent and

saluted. Vespasian gestured them to the table and Maximus spread the map in front of them.

'What do we do next, Maximus?'

The Camp Prefect cleared his throat. 'I have already ordered from Gaul the wood we require for the gates and towers at Lake Camp. The local trees are twisted and stunted and I can find no native wood that I believe will be suitable. Any wood from Gaul will come ready carpentered. Also the timber we need for the wharves and warehouses at Lagoon Harbour will be brought over by sea as soon as there is fine weather. Gaius should take his cohorts over as soon as possible to start clearing this area.' On the map in front of him he indicated a neck of land thrusting into the water. 'I believe the Tribune and Captain Rufius have chosen an excellent site where building will not be difficult. The Sixth Cohort will build a defence line at the end of this peninsula to protect the landing site. They will clear away any opposition and then survey and build a road the 5 miles to Lake Camp as quickly as possible. I suggest we construct it wide enough for one cart only; the returning empty carts can give way to the loaded carts during the building of our fortress.'

Vespasian nodded his agreement. Maximus continued, 'I shall march with the First and Second Cohorts straight to the Lake Camp site and start preparatory work.'

'What about the enemy at Hengistbury?' Titus asked, pointing to the fortified trading post at the mouth of the Stour. 'Isn't it dangerous to leave them in your rear?'

'Once we have cut them off, I am confident they will surrender,' said Vespasian. 'We cannot afford to waste time on a siege. We will isolate them instead.'

Gaius Postumus, frowning, pointed at the lagoon on the map. 'Why must we use ships at all?' he asked. 'The legion is quite used to marching these distances, and we could all get to this Lake Camp place by land.'

There was a long silence in the room and everyone

looked to Vespasian, who said nothing. Gaius Postumus began to feel uncomfortable and wished he had not spoken, but stubbornly he continued. 'These combined operations by land and sea – that is not the way of the legions. It never has been.'

'It is now,' said Vespasian.

Chapter 9
JOURNEY TO GAUL

Julius enjoyed working with Marcus Carinus who had now been given greater responsibility in charge of the First Cohort. He was a careful and conscientious officer who did not take unnecessary risks with his men. In the early part of the campaigning season, the First Cohort had helped build the road from Lagoon Harbour to Lake Camp. Vespasian and Maximus had agreed that this road did not need to be of the highest quality because, as the campaign moved west, the base near the lagoon would become redundant and the road would be little used. Some of the native inhabitants were brought in as unwilling labourers for the backbreaking work of shovelling dirt and rocks as the legionaries stood guard to protect their progress from hostile raiders. Within 4 days the first carts were rolling through to the site chosen by Maximus for Lake Camp on the River Stour. Carinus, after consulting with Gaius Postumus, decided at the same time to construct a rampart across the neck of the peninsula on which Lake Camp was sited, partly to protect the base from attack, but mainly to prevent pilfering from the mountain of stores that would shortly build up there.

Maximus had marched with the Second Cohort and was already at Lake Camp when Julius came through with the first load of building material. He had marked out the outlines for the walls of the fortress and had decided where the aqueduct was to come from the Stour to bring water to the camp. Gangs of men were digging ditches around the area that would become the camp and Julius noticed that soldiers had commandeered teams of local oxen to drag timber to the site. He knew that the setting up of a legionary fortress was a well-practised activity and what appeared to be chaotic confusion, like ants scurrying round a disturbed nest, would in a day or two become a defensive position that no local army could hope to challenge.

Maximus took Julius aside. 'The weak point in this campaign is the first half of our supply line. Although we can get draught animals and some wood locally, I have found nothing suitable in this area that can provide the timbers necessary for gates and towers. I have already asked for these to be prepared in Gaul and the Fourth Legion stationed there have orders to find us sufficient grain and cattle to provide adequate supplies for the legion through next winter. We certainly will be able to squeeze a little corn from the natives here but not sufficient for nearly a thousand extra mouths. As you used to be with the Fourth, I want you to go back to Chichester and then to sail to the Haven in Gaul. There you must set up a supply chain that will not fail us. Don't come back here until you know that everything is organised or our campaign will grind to a halt.' Maximus handed Julius a scroll with details of all the supplies he required and the equipment he had already ordered.

Julius looked doubtful. 'I understand, Sir, but as a tribune I have little authority over generals or even local contractors.'

'That is easily resolved,' said Maximus. He handed Julius a leather wallet. 'In here is an authorisation signed by General Vespasian which should be sufficient for most occasions. If anyone still questions your orders there is also in here a letter signed and sealed by the Emperor Claudius himself giving the bearer imperial authority. Only use that if you have to. Guard them well, and return them to me when you have finished the job.'

Julius rode back to Lake Camp and found a boat that would take him to Chichester on the first stage of his journey. As his galley left the lagoon he noticed that soldiers were constructing beacons on either side of the narrow entrance, and when he landed at Chichester he found Rufius who explained that he had recommended the idea to Maximus to assist captains trying to make the harbour for the first time. These beacons would be constantly manned and would be lit during fogs and one hour before dusk every day. 'Tell all the supply captains that they should have no difficulty entering the lagoon as long as the tide is on the make and they are dead centre between the two beacons.'

When Julius landed at the Haven, he found that Maximus had done his preliminary work well. Some of the timbers were already waiting on the quayside and cart loads more arrived every day. Julius ordered that the timber should be the first thing to be shipped over to Britain and briefed the captains of the supply ships who were to make the crossing for the first time. The commander of the Fourth Legion had already received his instructions and was supportive, though he grumbled at the number of cattle he was required to supply. Julius had no need to use the letter from the Emperor, which lay unopened at the bottom of his pouch.

By mid-summer he felt there was nothing more he could achieve in Gaul. A steady supply of stores was rolling onto the quayside at the Haven, and the Roman vessels were efficiently shuttling back and forth to Britain. After he had checked and double-checked that everything was in order Julius decided it was time for him to rejoin the Second Legion.

Chapter 10
BATTLE FOR HOD HILL

It was midsummer and the two Roman generals were on horseback surveying the Celtic fort of Hod, which rose impressively in front of them. Vespasian and Titus were on the high ground to the east of Hod Hill and had a clear view of the enemy encampment. Half a mile further north was a second hill, equally defended by ramparts and ditches. This they had heard was called Ham. Together the two hills made a formidable obstacle. Behind both hills to the west ran the Stour with an escarpment rising steeply from the river to the fort walls. The original planners of these fortresses had used the natural features well for maximum security with minimum effort.

Vespasian had ridden up the Stour valley from Lake Camp with a small bodyguard that morning. He congratulated his brother on the success of his campaign so far. 'Your victory at the White Rings was magnificent. It had the desired effect and the fortress at Hengistbury surrendered to the Second Cohort without a fight.' He pointed to the daunting defences in front of them. 'These look to be a tougher nut though.' Titus started to explain how he was intending to launch his assault, but Vespasian stopped him. 'First you had better read this.' He handed his brother a sealed scroll.

'Do you know what it says?' Titus asked.

Vespasian nodded. Titus broke the seal and quickly read the document. 'I have been elected Consul in Rome for next year. I am to return home immediately to prepare to take up my duties.'

'I know,' said Vespasian. 'My congratulations, brother. I am relieving you of your position with immediate effect and I will give you a commander's escort for the journey back to Marseilles. The Emperor will have a ship waiting there. I have appointed Poenius Gaius Postumus as the next senior officer to lead this campaign.'

'Gaius Postumus!' Titus exploded. 'He couldn't lead a donkey. You won't have a fierce wind with him, more of a wet fart.' He stomped away then turned back to his brother and said more calmly, 'At least let me capture this hill. The men know me and will follow me. I will go back to Rome content if you let me finish the job here.'

Vespasian thought for a moment. 'All right, your command finishes in 3 days. I think the people of Rome can spare you that long. You will be months late in taking up your consulship anyhow. As for Gaius, I know he is a cautious man, but he is a good soldier. Once we have captured Hod, the major fighting for these cohorts is over and it will be mainly a question of organizing supplies and garrisoning the forts you have captured. He can do the tidying up well enough for the rest of this campaign. Next year the major thrust will be in the south and I will lead that myself.'

The two men tapped their horses into a walk and, keeping out of range of any weapons hurled from the walls, they started to look for weak spots in the defences. The fort at Hod was impressively defended. There were two banks of ramparts and ditches, with a wooden palisade on the top bank. It was from behind this wall that the enemy were shouting and jeering at the officers. 'Which is it to be first, Hod or Ham?' Vespasian asked.

'I believe Ham is slightly smaller and less well defended,' answered Titus. 'The cohort could probably crack that in a day or two, but their defeat would be unlikely to have any effect on the defenders in Hod. They obviously feel quite safe behind their walls. On the other hand, if we capture Hod, I cannot see Ham holding out any longer. Therefore I favour going for Hod. I doubt if they have a huge amount of supplies in there, particularly water. We discovered in White Rings that they had well-stocked water ponds, but these would only last a few weeks. We could certainly starve them out with a simple siege without risking any casualties, but that does not fit with your overall strategy.'

Titus stopped to see if Vespasian disagreed with his analysis so far. When Vespasian said nothing, he continued. 'If we try a frontal attack on the eastern walls we will lose many men. The main rampart is 15 ft high with a ditch 40 ft wide and an additional 15 ft deep between the two lines of defence. This means our men will be silhouetted as they come over the first wall and exposed in a killing ground between the two walls well in range of thrown missiles. Whoever designed this knew about war. Instead, I favour a direct assault on the south-west gate at first light tomorrow in the usual way. I will send in a diversionary force to the north-east entrance with orders to make as much noise as possible. That should draw off most of the defenders. The attack group will split into three. The left and right troops will attack the ramparts and ditches either side of the gate, while the soldiers in the centre will force the gate itself with scaling ladders. It worked well enough at White Rings, and I don't see why it shouldn't work again here.'

Vespasian nodded his approval of these tactics and Titus issued a rapid string of orders to his officers.

Vespasian said to his brother, 'I accept that I have asked you to command here, but I would be honoured if you would let me lead the men who are to attack the gate.'

'Too risky,' Titus answered. 'The Augusta cannot afford to lose both Flavian brothers at the same time.' He smiled. 'Nice try, though.'

Vespasian was not prepared to give up yet. 'I led the

German horsemen across the River Medway and turned round that battle. The men have got to know that their officers are prepared to fight whenever they ask them to fight. I will take care; it's not as if I am looking for the golden crown for the first man over the wall. After all, brother, I did accede to your request for you to see through this battle.'

'All right,' Titus reluctantly agreed under his younger brother's persuasion and the two of them in high spirits returned to the legion's marching camp to prepare for the next day.

The south-western entrance was a complicated arrangement of interlocking ramparts and causeways that made a direct assault on the gate impossible. In addition, as the land fell away steeply towards the river, an attack on a broad front was difficult. Vespasian had arranged with the centurions in charge of the two flanking movements that they would attack first to clear the path and Vespasian and the 50 men of his commando group would follow when the way was opened. Titus had insisted that two soldiers from the auxiliaries, Novak and Goran, were to act as the General's bodyguard, and privately he had instructed them that Vespasian was not to be allowed to climb the assault ladders. Novak was from Lusitania. He was a worrier and was concerned what might happen to him if Vespasian chose to disobey his brother's order. Goran had no such concerns. He was an amiable giant of a man from the Roman province of Dalmatia. His philosophy, if you could call such crude thinking a philosophy, was to do whatever seemed best at the time. As the sky began to lighten the attack groups lay silent and hidden. Only when the diversion at the north gate was well established would they advance.

'They should be starting any time now,' Vespasian

whispered to the two centurions who lay beside him on the turf. As he spoke a mighty noise swelled from the north wall of the camp.

For five long minutes more his attacking force lay hidden and then Vespasian gave the order to go. The two columns snaked forward, to be met with shouts and abuse from the walls in front of them. This was not the surprise attack they had hoped for. The Romans yelled back as they rushed up the grass banks with their swords drawn, holding their shields in front of them.

At the top of the bank a hail of missiles met the attackers and the centurion immediately gave the order to form the *testudo* or tortoise. Hours of practice on the drill ground now showed their benefit. The soldiers instantly created a huddle. Those in the centre held their long battle shields above their heads, covering their companions. Those on the flanks provided similar protection for their comrades. The tortoise crept forward, now impervious to the rain of stones and arrows from above. Their responsibility was to defend the ladder men as they started to climb the walls.

The tortoise reached the gate undamaged and, when he saw this, Vespasian ordered his small force to move. The ladder men pushed forward, only to discover that the defensive towers either side of the gates meant that the tortoise was unable to provide them with the necessary protection. Almost immediately, ladder men found themselves exposed to an assault of stones and arrows. While enemy spearmen lined the ramparts to prevent anyone reaching the top, slingers were raining shots on the climbers from platforms that were angled almost behind the Romans.

Two ladders were successfully in position when Vespasian was caught on the side of the head by a rock, hurled from one of the towers. He stumbled and fell to the ground. The Celts, who had targeted him as one of the commanders, let out a cheer. Novak and Goran stood

71

astride the General's body to give him protection. Both held up their long legionary's shields to ward off further missiles and Goran roared to the other soldiers for assistance. The ladders were abandoned and the impetus of the attack was held. The legionaries either sought protection from the bombardment for themselves or came over to make a protective ring around the fallen Vespasian.

A sally out from the gates at this moment might have serious consequences and Titus, watching the attack closely, decided that this action was not going to succeed and his brother was in serious danger. He signalled a squadron of heavy cavalry from the auxiliaries in to rescue Vespasian and ordered the trumpeter to sound the fall back. The sound was echoed from the north of the fortress. The Celts cheered their triumph as the force of Romans retreated in disarray with their wounded.

The surgeon was putting stitches into Vespasian's head when Titus came to find him. Titus was remarkably cheerful. 'Well, that wasn't very successful was it? I think we rather underestimated the resolve of the defenders and the cleverness of the defences. Those slingers coming in from behind you was a very effective move. That confused us and slowed us down. Actually I doubt if you would have managed to climb the gates even if you hadn't been knocked down.'

A much-subdued Vespasian grimaced as the surgeon tied the last of the stitches. 'Thank you for the rescue,' he muttered.

Titus called forward the two soldiers who had accompanied him 'These are the two you should be thanking.' He introduced Novak and Goran who looked decidedly uncomfortable.

Vespasian did thank them and wondered how he might suitably reward them. After some thought, it came to him what would go down well with the other auxiliaries. 'I am granting Roman citizenship to both of you. You are now eligible to join the Legion proper. In addition, both of you will be awarded the *corona civica*.' This was a wreath that was only given to those who save the life of another Roman soldier. To wear the corona was a privilege that would be acknowledged by all Roman soldiers in every legion.

Vespasian continued, 'I would also like the two of you to join my staff as my permanent bodyguard.'

Novak accepted immediately, seeing this as a comfortable alternative to life in the front line. Goran looked less certain. 'Will there be as much fighting as being in the Legion?' he asked. When Vespasian assured him that as a general he always intended to be in the middle of any fighting that was going on, Goran agreed readily. Vespasian turned to talk to his brother as the two new Roman citizens stood awkwardly, uncertain what to do next. When the General at last dismissed them they were relieved to leave the sick-bay as neither had any previous experience of talking to officers.

'While you have been lying idly here in the hospital tent, I have been making further plans,' Titus said. 'I have sent to Maximus at Lake Camp for two of the onagars and more ballistas. We should not have attempted this assault without adequate artillery. The carpenters are building a tower near the eastern wall, which I want to be 50 ft high. It will take 3 days to get everything ready. I trust you will give me one extra day of my command.'

Vespasian found his brother's enthusiasm infectious and his low spirits evaporated. The two left the hospital tent discussing what had gone wrong and planning the next attack on Hod.

Two days of frantic work later the tower was completed. A company of 20 horsemen arrived that morning from Lake Camp accompanying four mules. These carried the ballistas and ammunition. The ballista was a powerful crossbow on a wooden frame whose ammunition was rocks, metal bolts or wooden-shafted arrows, propelled by a twisted strip of leather. It was useless in wet weather as the leather became saggy, but in dry weather it was very effective and could also be used to fire with considerable accuracy.

The centurion in charge said the onagars were coming by cart and should be at the camp by nightfall. The artillerymen reported to Titus and were given their instructions. They hoisted two of the ballistas up to the platform on top of the tower. From there they had a clear view over the walls into the fortress of Hod. They could see one large house in the centre and over a hundred huts straggling down a main street. All the huts had thatched roofs. Titus had told these men that the next day he wanted a rain of fire on the centre of the settlement. The officer in charge set the ballistas to shoot in an arc of 45 degrees; then they waited.

Just before dusk the cart pulled by four oxen trundled into camp. Titus ordered the onagars to be taken straight away to a site near the south gate and set up. Over the last 2 days the soldiers had collected a vast pile of rocks, which were to be the ammunition for next day's attack.

The onagar was built on a solid wooden frame with four axled wheels to allow the specialist crew to manoeuvre the catapult around to direct fire where ordered. A long lever was wound back by twisting a rope on a ratchet and, when released, it could hurl a large rock 100 paces. It was named after the onagars, the wild donkeys of North Africa, because the soldiers said it had a kick like an ass.

With all preparations complete and the weapons well guarded the soldiers lay down to grab what sleep they could.

The attack when it came the next day was brutal. Within minutes the rain of fiery bolts had set the central huts ablaze. From his position on the tower Titus could see Celts running screaming from their houses. Some  tried desperately to put out the fires, others to drag the burning straw from their roofs, but this was useless as they just found themselves in danger from the next volley of flaming ammunition.

Titus pointed out one figure who was obviously issuing orders to the other defenders on the hill. Both ballista captains loaded their weapons with metal bolts and carefully trained them on the man over 150 paces distant. Both were confident that it would be their ballista that would hit him. They fired on Titus's command and there was noisy celebration from the tower as the figure was seen to jerk and fall like a puppet whose strings had been cut. Titus hastily reassured both crews that they would be equally credited with the kill and ordered them to continue the destruction. He then left the tower and returned to his command post. To the south, a cheer from the crews occasionally interrupted the regular thud of rocks hitting the ramparts as one of their missiles hit the gate work.

After half an hour Titus ordered the ballistas to stop firing as the defenders were now hiding from the Romans' obvious deadly accuracy, but the onagars thumped on all morning. The majority of the rocks could not be sufficiently accurately aimed to bring quick success, but after midday

Titus again mounted the tower to see what damage had been achieved. One of the gates was completely splintered and the other was forced loose from its gatepost. Already there was sufficient space for an attacking force to get through.

He ordered firing to stop and sent a volunteer forward to speak to the defenders. Not many minutes later a forlorn delegation could be seen picking their way over the tumble of rocks and the interpreter brought them to Titus. The negotiations were speedy. Titus offered all inhabitants safe passage from the camp in return for immediate surrender. To be spared, all had to leave the camp and one in every ten of them would be sent to Rome as slaves. By 4 o'clock a steady stream of men, women and children struggled out of the wrecked gateway carrying what they could of their possessions.

Soldiers separated the healthy and young to be sent to Rome as slaves. The others drifted off into the nearby woods.

'Where will they go now?' Titus asked.

'That's their problem, not mine,' was Vespasian's blunt reply. Before nightfall the legion had moved into Hod.

The following day Vespasian embraced his brother and wished him a safe journey. 'Thank you for this victory at Hod. Not only has it cost us no lives, but also it has shown the other tribes that resistance to the Roman army will come to nothing. I shall build a legionary camp inside Hod and use it for my base to secure the upper Stour. Next year we will use what we have learned here on our journey westwards. May the gods protect you brother. Now go and sort out Rome.'

With that the brothers embraced again and Titus rode off for Richborough and home.

Chapter 11
STRANGER ON THE HILL

It was a holiday. The mid-August sun burned hot on their naked bodies. Dirk and Dug ran screaming over the river bank and tumbled each other like puppies splashing and playing in the warm water. Higher up the River Frome Conn and Huw threw their net one more time and collected two small fish meshed in its folds. These were added to the basket submerged among the reeds at the edge of the river. They agreed they had done enough for the time being and threw themselves down on the grassy bank to dry off in the heat of the sun. In the cloudless sky they watched the pipits soar up and parachute back down to the grass meadow. Unseen by both of them an otter gently plopped into the water, no doubt on its own fishing expedition, and disappeared upstream. Tiny blue butterflies flitted around them and settled on the long grass stems. Mai-dun in the distance shimmered in the heat and looked impregnable and safe.

The bean harvest and the corn crop would be ready for gathering in the next week and the whole community would be working every hour of daylight. Kareth had given Conn permission to go to the river as long as he brought fish back for them. Silda had agreed that Huw could go too if he took the twins along. The two elder boys could hear the twins shouting in the distance. Lazily they discussed where their future might lie in Mai-dun, though carefully neither of them mentioned Morwen.

It was Huw who noticed first that it was a while since they had heard any noise from Dirk and Dug. They ran downstream expecting the usual disaster from the twins. As they came to a broad curve in the river where they had left the boys, to their relief they saw them both safe on the bank. They were struggling to put their clothes on while talking to a stranger. Huw ran up ready to protect his brothers and with no preliminary greetings demanded, 'Who are you? What do you want?' Conn arrived and put a cautionary hand on his friend's arm. He had immediately noticed that the man was grey with tiredness. His right arm hung useless at his side and he looked ready to collapse.

'Come, sit down here,' Conn suggested gently. 'It's time we ate.' The man almost stumbled as he lowered himself to the grass and winced with pain as his weight was taken on his right side. No one knew what to say, so it was in silence that Conn broke the loaf of bread in pieces and handed it round with some strips of dried meat. The man ate as if he had not seen food for days. Conn gave his drinking bowl to Dug who went to the river and brought it back for the stranger to drink from.

'Where are you from?' the man asked.

'From Mai-dun,' Huw answered, pointing at the hill 2 miles away.

The man took a swig of water. 'My name is Rohan and I used to live at Hod.' There was a pause as Huw and Conn digested this information. They had heard of Hod, a fortress to rival Mai-dun in size, but too far away to be an enemy. Conn broke the silence by telling Rohan their names.

There was another long gap in the conversation as the boys searched for their next question. Then Dirk piped up. 'What's the matter with your arm?'

'I think it's broken,' Rohan replied. With his left hand he struggled to remove his shirt and expose his right side. His upper arm was badly discoloured with black and yellow bruising and an egg-size bump just above the elbow. He peeled off a rough bandage from the lower arm revealing a deep and jagged cut that was still oozing blood. The boys were quite used to seeing injuries, and they were more impressed by the cut than by the obviously broken arm.

'How did that happen?' asked Dug, pointing to the open wound.

'The Romans came to Hod and there was a battle which we lost.' He started to tell them about the rumours his people had heard early in the year and of the arrival of the soldiers. The twins were gripped by the story, but Huw and Conn exchanged a quick glance. They had both realised that this was information that should be shared with the Council of Elders, particularly with Bannoc.

'You must come back to Mai-dun,' Huw said. 'The Teacher can fix your arm and you can sleep with us. My father is Captain of the Slingers.' He spoke with quiet authority and for once neither the twins nor Conn, who usually questioned everything Huw said, thought to argue his decision. It was agreed that Conn would run back to collect the net and the fish while the others crossed the river by the ford just downstream and they would meet up on the way back to the settlement. Conn caught up with the little group just short of the first ditch and together they climbed the hill and entered by the east gate. Rolf and Silda were both at home and all four of the boys led Rohan like a trophy into the hut.

Everyone was talking at once except Rohan who was standing slumped in the doorway. Silda, noticing his distress, led him to a pile of rugs near the fire and invited him to sit down. She gently eased him onto the rugs while Rolf called for quiet. He invited Huw to explain what had happened which the boy managed to do with only occasional interruptions from his brothers. Rohan's shirt was removed once more and Silda tutted over the condition of his arm. Rolf listened intently and then indicated to everyone once more to be quiet.

'Rohan, you are welcome as a guest in my home. Morwen, go and ask the Teacher if he will come here to advise us what to do with this arm.' Turning to Huw he said, 'Find Bannoc and tell him what has happened. Say to him that Rohan must rest now, but he will be able to come to a meeting of the Council by sun-down.' He looked at the twins. 'You two go and collect buckets of water and bring them back to your mother. Then you can go and play.' The twins looked disappointed, but Rolf added, 'Rohan is going to sleep now. There will be plenty of time later for stories.'

Silda fetched a large wicker-work basket from the back of the hut. 'Conn, take the fishes you caught to Kareth. When Morwen returns with Maddoc, I need the two of you to collect some of the eating plants that I have pointed out to her down by the stream.' She handed him the basket and took him outside the hut. 'I am depending on you to protect her. These are difficult times. Take this.' She handed him a short dagger in a worn leather sheath. 'Look after it as it belongs to Rolf.'

'Will he mind me having his knife?' Conn asked nervously.

'Rolf trusts you,' Silda answered. 'We all trust you. Look after her well.'

When Silda and Rolf had successfully managed to get all the children out of the hut, Rolf turned to Rohan. 'I don't want you to talk any more until you have seen the Elders. Maddoc will dress your arm, then you must sleep.' He turned to Silda. 'The man must be hungry. Make some hot food for him.' As the various parties returned from their errands Rolf told each of them they were not to return to the hut for some time. Morwen left to find Conn, and Huw, realising his sister and best friend did not require his company on this occasion, went off to tell his story to some of the other young slingers. The twins collected friends and made for the Mai-dun grass ramparts and played happily at Romans and Celts, a game that involved a lot of shouting and rolling down the banks.

After some minutes Maddoc arrived carrying a small wooden box. He crouched down next to Rohan and ran his fingers up and down the damaged area, taking his time prodding and squeezing Rohan's upper arm, which made his patient wince. 'This I will try to straighten and splint. The bone should mend, but your injured arm will always be weaker than the other.' He pointed to the open wound. 'How many days since this was done?'

'Five days,' Rohan answered.

'That is too long really,' Maddoc said. 'I will try to pin the sides together with thorns after I have cleaned away some of the dried blood, though I don't know how well the sides will knit. You will be fortunate if it doesn't turn rotten, but I will use my best skill. I will bandage the wound with chickweed which should keep it clean.' He asked Rohan to tell his story again and listened intently while he worked. Rohan finished the telling at much the same time as Maddoc finished binding the wound. Maddoc drew a little clay pot from out of his box. 'I will give you three drops of poppy juice which will help you to sleep now. Tonight you must tell your story to our Chief.'

In the late afternoon sun Conn and Morwen were walking slowly along the bank of the little stream. She was carrying the basket already half full of leaves and flowers, and Conn was wearing the knife strapped to his waist. Morwen was giving Conn a lesson on edible plants. 'Try this.' She bent down and picked some pale green leaves. 'Go on, eat it; it's all right.' She fed him one of the leaves, which he chewed on. 'That's poppy. Maddoc uses the juice from the seeds for medicine, but we like the leaves for eating.' They walked on a bit further. 'There is a myrtle bush. Maddoc doesn't know about that one. I almost told him of it when he sent you down to the Frome at the time of the mysteries.' The boy and girl strolled on in companionable silence beside the ancient willow trees that stood along the riverbank like old ladies dipping their feet in the water. From time to time Morwen pointed out different plants, teaching Conn their names and how they could be used. She indicated some pale blue flowers growing among the long grass. 'Pull up one of those carefully.'

Conn did so and shook the earth from the fat roots. 'Are these for supper?'

'I hope not. That's cow-bane. Though some people use it in medicines, it's very poisonous. If you eat those roots you die. One drop of that yellow sap and you will have stomach ache.' Conn threw the plant away and went to rinse his hands in the stream. There was a rustling from the alder bushes on the far bank and he quickly drew his dagger out of the sheath. A roe deer sprang from the cover and darted and zigzagged up the hill. Morwen laughed and teased him. 'My protector!' But Conn beckoned her across the stream. Hidden by the lowest fronds of the bushes was a young fawn. Its eyes were wide with fear, but it stayed completely still, hoping its camouflage would keep it safe.

Conn held back the branches and bent to pick it up. 'This skin will make a soft pair of shoes for you, Morwen,' he said.

'Leave it,' Morwen spoke sharply. Conn stepped back and looked questioningly at the girl. She continued more gently, 'If you pick it up the mother will not return and the fawn will certainly be eaten by wolves tonight. If we go now she will come back and then it has a chance.' She struggled to find the right words for an idea that was in her head. 'It has done us no harm and has as much right to life as we have. Let's leave it alone.' This was a new thought for Conn, but seeing how anxious she was, he dropped the branches and together they crossed back over the stream and finding a grassy bank sat down in the evening sunshine.

'I'm glad I didn't kill the fawn,' Conn said. 'I don't much like the idea of killing. It's like you said, the animal has done us no harm.'

'A fine soldier you'll make,' Morwen said with a laugh. She lay back and closed her eyes. Running her hand through the grass she suddenly felt a sharp jab. 'Ow, that hurt,' she said and sitting up she sucked the small drop of blood from her finger. The two of them searched the grass to see what had caused this and Conn found a small bronze pin brooch, half buried in the soil. The pin itself was crudely made, but on it a bronze claw clasped a piece of amber delicately incised with a human figure. He went down to the water to wash it in the stream and returning he knelt beside the girl. Using a stone he blunted the sharp point and carefully fastened the pin to her dress. Morwen placed her hand over the brooch. 'I shall keep this, and remember this moment for ever,' she said.

The two of them sat back on the bank and Conn picked at a dull green plant growing between them. He held it up to Morwen's nose. 'What is this one?'

'That's thyme,' she answered. 'My mother uses it to flavour meat.' She lay back on the grass, silent for a while, and then said, 'You know I would like to be wed to you, Conn, but it is not possible.' She paused to let her words sink in. 'My father wants me to marry into one of the leaders' families; someone like Serap.' She mentioned a young man of Huw's age whose father had been one of the Elders.

Conn looked sad but not surprised. 'I quite like Serap,' he said after a while. 'I have always known I cannot marry you, Morwen.' He paused. 'I probably won't marry anyone.' He stretched out his hand to her and their fingers entwined.

Morwen continued speaking slowly. 'You know that man who you brought here today? What he said frightened me. Do you remember the time we helped Maddoc with the mysteries, what he told us? *There's a strong wind coming over our land, which is going to blow our people away. It's going to be a time of sorrow for the people.* Do you think what Rohan told us has something to do with that?'

'I'm not sure. I think it must have been a Roman spy who gave me that cup. But don't be scared.' Conn got to his feet and held out his two hands. She took hold of these and he gently pulled her to her feet. 'Even if I cannot marry you, remember, I'm your protector, officially appointed by your mother, and I'll even carry your basket home.' His cheerfulness eased her worries, and they set off back home hand in hand.

That evening Rolf escorted Rohan to Bannoc's hut. Many of the people stared at them as they walked up the main street, but no one dared address them directly. Inside the house Bannoc and Maddoc were waiting with Garth, the commander of the warriors, and other members of Maidun's Council. Bannoc's woman gestured to Rolf and Rohan to sit and handed round cups of mead. Rohan started to tell his story for the fourth time. The assembled group listened in silence.

Earlier in the year the people of Hod had heard of the Roman army landing by the lake some miles to the south, and had also heard stories about the building of a new fortress on the lower reaches of the *Isca Stour,* but they were confident that they were safe behind their massive walls. The chieftains at Hod and at the nearby fort at Ham had agreed to work together and they had strengthened their walls and collected additional thorn bushes, which were usually sufficient to deter attackers. Then they made certain their water pits and food stores were as full as possible. They heard that the people of White Rings had surrendered to the invaders, but inside Hod they still felt confident that no attacker would think it worthwhile to bother with such a formidably defended position.

Just before the summer turning of the year the Roman army had appeared and the Chief had ordered the gates to be closed. About 700 attackers camped on the high ground to the east of Hod. Rohan described the first assault and how he and the other slingers had defended the southern entrance. The Roman commander had nearly been captured and everyone celebrated when the attackers turned and fled. They expected the enemy at this point to leave. He went on to describe the building of the tower and then the rain of death from the fiery arrows. Rohan had to tell the story of this attack again after detailed questioning from Garth. The Chieftain was killed when his hut was set on fire, but the fighters still felt they could defend the perimeter from direct assault. Rohan then described the relentless pounding as great rocks flew at the river gateway.

'Hour after hour the great gates were hammered until one burst inwards and the other was knocked away from the supporting post. Without our leader, the people started to panic. Those who had been part of the Council, at least those who were still alive, met together and quickly arrived at the decision that further resistance would serve no purpose. When the barrage stopped a Roman soldier came forward to speak to us. The acting chief had no spirit and we agreed to surrender. Very quickly the whole community was called together and carrying our injured we all left by the River Gate.'

Garth wanted to know every detail about the attack, and Rohan told him the little he knew, trying to describe the horrors of the assault and the devastation caused. Garth continued to question him in particular about the catapult, about its range, the size of stones and the frequency of fire. He learned a little, but Rohan was not a good enough soldier to have noted the details of such things. Rolf wanted to know how the slingers had protected the gates. Here Rohan was able to provide an eyewitness description.

'How did you escape?' asked Maddoc.

'I heard that those who surrendered at White Rings had been taken prisoner and were no longer in our country. I had no wish to become a slave. Just outside the gate I decided to try to break free but was caught by a Roman sword on my arm here.' He pointed to his bandaged arm. 'The blow knocked me over and I fell down the steep slope to the *Isca Stour*. As I fell, I caught my arm on one of the rocks and felt the bone break. I reached the river and fell in. I don't think anyone chased me, but with a broken arm I felt certain I'd drown. I drifted downstream until the river became shallow enough to wade across. I wanted to get as far away from the Romans as possible, but I have been wandering around lost for 4 days until I met your young people this morning.'

The men who made up the Council of Elders talked quietly among themselves. Bannoc then turned to Rohan and asked, 'Can these Romans be beaten?'

'It is impossible to beat them in battle, there are too many of them. But if you could stop the gates being battered down, and if you could protect yourselves from the arrows, then I think your walls could be defended.'

'We thank you for everything you have told us,' Bannoc acknowledged. 'Now we must discuss it further. You are welcome to stay in Mai-dun until you have mended from your injuries. The people will look after you. When you are better, you may either join our community or go on your way. The choice is yours. Now, please leave us to our talks.'

The Council talked late into the night. Garth was for mounting a defence whatever the cost, but Bannoc was more concerned for the survival of the people. However, he was also aware that if the community at Mai-dun ceased to exist so did his authority. Maddoc largely kept quiet, remembering the vision he had had at the time of the mysteries. Eventually, all were in agreement and Bannoc decided to call the people together at the end of the working day.

There were nearly a thousand people sitting on the grass at the meeting place. Bannoc recounted to them all that Rohan had told the Elders yesterday. 'Your leaders have talked about this and we believe that we can defeat these Romans; not by battle, but by defending our homes as your ancestors have done at Mai-dun for hundreds of years. These Romans will not come this year, but sometime in the spring. We will be ready for them.' There was a growl of approval from the men.

'Some of you will decide to leave between now and then. I cannot stop you. For those of us who stay there will be hard work this winter. The ditches must be deepened and the walls strengthened. More chesils must be collected from the beach for the slingers and we must dig extra ponds to hold water. We will not defeat this enemy by sitting and doing nothing. All boys over the age of 12 must train for fighting.' Conn looked across at Huw and grinned. 'This work will start as soon as the harvest is collected. Everything must be ready by the time of next season's sowing.'

Chapter 12
THE ROAD MAKERS

Julius arrived back in Britain around mid-summer, after his time in Gaul. He travelled in one of the supply galleys, which were all arriving at the temporary wharves of Lagoon Harbour. His ship had to join a queue of others waiting to unload. A centurion, in charge of disembarkation, was vainly shouting orders at everyone in earshot. Every day he had to organise the unloading of goods from Gaul, the dispatch of supplies to Lake Camp, the building of a second wharf and the defence of the whole complex. At that moment he was dealing with three angry sea captains anxious to get their ships tied up and secure at the end of a hazardous sea voyage. Julius decided not to wait, and jumping across the two boats ahead of him in the queue, he used his authority to acquire a horse and set off to ride the 5 miles to Lake Camp. He was pleased to see that transport on the new road was working well. The returning empty carts pulled into lay-bys off the narrow surfaced road to allow the laden carts through and the road traffic was moving smoothly.

When he arrived at Lake Camp he found the fortress nearly completed. He reported to Maximus and answered all his questions to reassure him that a steady stream of supplies was coming from Gaul. Julius also mentioned the developing chaos at Lagoon Harbour, and Maximus decided to go there immediately to use his authority to sort things out. 'You have done well, Tribune,' Maximus said to him. 'Now report to Marcus Carinus and the First Cohort. If you follow the line of our new road westwards, you should find them. Remind Carinus I require him to push forward with all speed.'

Julius set off early next morning on the horse he had commandeered from Lagoon Harbour. He realised he had forgotten to hand back to Maximus the leather wallet that contained the signatures of Vespasian and the Emperor, but thought there would be time enough for that later. The road, of course, was straight, but he was impressed with the well-engineered camber and the carefully graded surface. This was not a road built solely for conquest; this was for settlement. He noted how far the trees had been felled on either side to provide a security strip for travellers. It was a fine sunny morning and he chewed on a biscuit as his horse trotted on. After he had been riding for an hour he had reason to be grateful for the caution of the Roman engineers. He saw a group of four raggedy Celts come out of the woods on his right who threatened him with shouts and stones. One rock landed on the roadway immediately in front of his horse, which made it skitter sideways, but the group was too far away to cause him real concern. He quickened his horse's pace and left them behind.

Nine miles down the road he came to the first signs of road building. Groups of local tribesmen, supervised by Roman soldiers, were collecting stones from the ditches on either side and hammering them into the road surface. Julius pulled his horse to a halt next to one of the legionaries who gave him a smart salute. 'Where can I find the senior officer, soldier?'

'Centurion Carinus is about a mile ahead, Sir, up the road. There has been some trouble with one of the work gangs and he has gone to sort it out.' Julius rode on. The surface of the road was now rougher and in front of him he could see the trees closing in. He found Carinus who had already sorted out the little local difficulty and reported to him. It felt good to be back with the First Cohort and he and Carinus sat down on a tree trunk together and shared a jug of wine.

Julius passed on Maximus's parting instruction about speed. 'Not again,' growled Carinus. 'I get that instruction every day. We can't go any faster than we're doing. Already I'm pushing forward nearly a mile every day. Any faster and our soldiers will be too thinly spread and in danger from attack.' Julius told him about the small group who had accosted him along the road. 'That's what I mean,' said Carinus. 'I won't put my men at any greater risk.' Julius felt he had passed on his message and he didn't need to do anything further, because it was obvious that the road making was pushing forward at an impressive pace.

Carinus continued, 'There's a young friend of yours up at the road head, the Greek surveyor Alexis. He is doing excellent work. Find yourself a billet in camp and you will see him this evening.' Julius asked if he could go on and meet him immediately and Carinus gave his permission.

It was a great pleasure for Julius to meet up with Alexis again and the two friends embraced. Alexis had been in charge of surveying the line the road would take through the woods and Julius was impressed at the authority the young Greek had over such a large number of legionaries and auxiliaries in the construction gangs. Over 100 men were working together on a complicated road-making movement. Alexis, standing in the middle of what would be the new road, explained what was going on to Julius. He pointed out a column of smoke in the distance. 'That's my marker,' he said. 'I fixed that point a few days ago and there's a group of four soldiers standing by the fire on a little hill with orders to keep it burning at all times.'

He stuck his surveying pole into the centre of the roadway and lined up one of the arms with the column of smoke. 'If this was open country,' he explained, 'we would use signal flags instead of beacons. We will be through this woodland by tomorrow and then the work will be much faster.'

There followed a series of shouts and waving of flags to right and left and Julius could see that stakes were being driven into the ground. Alexis called him over. 'This arm,' he pointed to his pole, 'is lined up on the smoke and gives us our overall direction. These arms to left and right give us the line for the roadbed or causeway, what we call the *agger*. The auxiliaries are marking this with these posts.' He showed Julius a wooden stake 4ft high marked with the Second Legion's emblem of *capricornus*, the goat. 'This is our road and we want to be proud of it.' He shouted and waved his flag to his assistant 100 paces further on who hammered his stake into the ground. Alexis moved forward to the next pair of markers using a measuring chain of exactly 5 ft to find the centre of the roadway. Then he repeated the process.

'This is the way you Romans have built roads all over the world,' he said. 'One of my work gangs will clear the topsoil from the line of the *agger* we have just marked out. The chalk here is only 2 ft below this surface and so the trench does not need to be any deeper that. The other gangs dig ditches into the chalk on either side of the *agger* and collect any stones they find and throw them into the trench we have dug. Eventually we will have built up a causeway exactly 10 ft wide, and if I have done my job properly it will be as straight as an arrow's flight to our next beacon point.'

He smiled at his friend. 'There is a cavalry officer called Critus up ahead. His squadron is scouting and providing us with protection. If you would like to go and find him, get him to show you where our beacon is. The soldiers there will be pleased to see you, and if you look to the west you'll see something you will recognise.'

Julius said goodbye to his friend for the time being and rode down the line of markers and into the woods. He easily found Critus with his horsemen who told him that there were no enemy in the area. Julius felt it was safe to go on alone, and by following the smoke signal, after 15 minutes, he arrived at the foot of the little hill. He tied his horse to a tree and climbed up to greet the fire-watchers who were indeed pleased to see him. From the summit Julius was able to follow the line of the new road arrowing back to Lake Camp. To the south-east he could see the great pool by Lagoon Harbour and the site of the next fortress, Morionium. From his vantage point for the first time he felt he could understand the brilliance of Vespasian's campaign. When he looked west he could just make out the ramparts of Mai-dun shimmering in the sunlight. *Not this year*, he thought excitedly, *but early next spring we'll be there.*

Chapter 13
PREPARING FOR BATTLE

It was December and the Second Legion was once again in winter quarters, most of them in the new fortress at Lake Camp. Vespasian had ridden north with a strong bodyguard to Colchester to report to Aulus Plautius on the satisfactory progress of the campaign so far. Maximus was in command of the Augusta in his absence. Marcus Carinus and the First Cohort were securing the defences of Morionium, which would become the base for launching next season's assault up the River Frome. Vespasian had given instructions to Julius to sail back to the Reed Pool with 30 soldiers and had given him full authority. This small force was to avoid direct contact with the enemy wherever possible and Julius was to bring back a detailed plan of the defences of Mai-dun. Vespasian knew his forces were spread thinly over a large area, and he hoped the enemy were aware of the convention that the winter months were not the best time for fighting.

Julius asked permission from Carinus to take Alexis with him again. He suggested that together they could bring back some accurate drawings for the General to look at. He was still nervous about being in command and the idea of having an intelligent friend with him was an attractive one. With Alexis he could exchange ideas, something that was impossible for a Roman officer to do with the soldiers under him. Though reluctant to lose the young Greek even for a short while, Carinus recognised the value of the suggestion and readily agreed.

Julius's voyage west was no copy of their journey the previous year. A south-westerly gale threatened to crash the ship onto the chalk pillars soon after they left the safety of Lagoon Harbour. His new captain seemed to have little confidence in how to handle the rough seas and made things worse by keeping too close to the shore. Julius and many of the soldiers were seasick. To the disgust of his men, Julius ordered them to take a turn at the oars. However, the unusual activity and the degree of concentration necessary for rowing actually made them forget their stomachs. The ship crawled and crabbed its way clear of the cliffs to gain some sea room. Julius mentioned to the captain the safety to be found in the little cove he and Rufius had spotted on their first voyage and the galley shot through the bottleneck entrance to the calm waters inside. They beached on the pebbles and Julius told the captain that they would stay there until the storm had blown itself out. The soldiers were only too pleased to be on dry land and in the usual efficient legionary manner quickly set up a campsite where the grass met the pebbles.

The bad weather lasted for 3 days. On the fourth, with some reluctance, the soldiers abandoned the safety of their land base. They had not enjoyed the voyage so far and needed to be reassured by Julius that the journey by sea was not very much further. So it turned out. Rounding the headland Julius and Alexis recognised the site of their previous adventure. After a quick discussion they agreed that they should set up a base at least a mile to the east of their previous camp so that they could avoid the village that had caused them trouble before. Next morning Julius left the centurion in charge of a small detachment of 20 legionaries to keep watch on the ship and their encampment and set off with a guard of 10 soldiers. He ordered the captain to put to sea if his ship was in danger of being overwhelmed by natives.

At the same time as Julius was gathering information for Vespasian, Bannoc's plan for Mai-dun was being put into action. By mid-September the corn had been harvested, and Bannoc divided all the settlers above the age of 6 into four working parties. No one had taken the chance to leave the hill because the security and confidence of Mai-dun's defences seemed a better option than the near certainty of starvation outside. Garth was responsible with his group for deepening the ditches. Week after week the men and women dug down with their antler picks and filled baskets with earth and stone. They started with the innermost ditch and worked their way round the entire perimeter. Baskets were emptied into an ox cart and the spoil was taken to the east and west entrances. Bannoc himself was in charge of the largest group. Their task was to strengthen the defences around the gates. He had learned much from Rohan's description of the Roman assault on Hod. To defend the gates he built up additional walls shaped like the curve of oxen horns. He hoped these would keep the Roman catapults at sufficient distance to protect the Mai-dun gates from flying rocks. At the same time the defenders would be able to pour missiles on the sides and backs of any attackers. Rohan had decided to take his chances with the defenders of Mai-dun. As his broken arm had not fully recovered Bannoc asked him to supervise the collection of timbers and thorn bushes from outside the camp to fortify the top of the walls. The fourth group, led by Rolf, was building a series of heavily fortified wooden platforms every hundred paces round the summit of the hill to give protection to his slingers from the Roman missiles. Weak points in the defences were identified and systematically strengthened.

Just after the turn of the year Rolf told Bannoc that he would need to build up his supply of pebbles for the slingshots. He believed they had about 5,000 suitable missiles buried in pits around the hillfort, but he would like another 10,000 so that they would have sufficient ammunition to hold off the anticipated Roman attacks. When Rolf mentioned this at home Huw immediately volunteered for the task. Conn, who was fed up with humping earth, asked to go with him. Rolf gave them an ox cart and six baskets made of willow strips and told the boys to be careful, particularly as they would have to cross the Fleet lagoon to reach the chesil beach. Dirk and Dug implored their parents to be allowed to go along too and received permission. Morwen, however, had to remain at home as Silda told her that she was needed there.

The four boys packed some food and warm clothes and set off in high spirits. Conn, who knew best how to handle oxen, drove the cart. The others sometimes walked and sometimes hitched a lift inside the rickety vehicle. The little party laboured up to the top of the Ridgeway and then made good time downhill towards the sea. They headed for an area where Conn knew it was possible to wade across the channel at low tide to reach the pebble bank. When they arrived at the shore of the Fleet they sat down to eat their food.

Unfortunately none of them had thought how they could best get the stones from the beach across the water back to the mainland. Arguments flowed to and fro as each of them put in their suggestion. Conn reckoned he could drive the cart over to the other side at low water, load it up and then wait for the next low water to bring it back. Huw rejected this as too risky. He thought the heavily laden cart would probably stick in the mud and he did not relish having to explain this failure to his father. He was for carrying pebbles, a few at a time, across in the baskets. It was Dirk who came up with an answer that satisfied them all. After lunch they unhitched the cart and with Conn and Dirk riding one of the oxen and Huw and Dug the other, festooned with baskets, they urged the animals into the water and waded across. They quickly loaded two of the baskets with pebbles. These were tied to one of the oxen and Conn led it back across the freezing water. By the time he had emptied the stones into the cart and returned to the other side, the next oxen was loaded and he repeated the operation. After about an hour the tide was noticeably creeping higher and higher. Huw decided that it would be too risky to continue and all four of them crossed back to the mainland. There was nothing more they could do until low tide next morning so they decided to explore.

Near the mouth of the river the boys came across the fishing village that Julius and Alexis had found a year earlier. When Huw explained what they had been doing the headman invited them to sleep there and welcomed them to share their food. He told the boys that at dusk the villagers were going to hunt wild fowl and Conn asked him if they could join in. The headman readily agreed, but told them they must be quiet or the birds would be scared off.

As the sun began to drop, four punts set off from the village and headed for the reed pool. Conn and Dirk accompanied the headman who lay in the bows with a net while one of the young villager boys pushed the boat along with a pole. Huw and Dug were in a second punt and these two separated from the others and headed to the north end of the pool, making a wide circle. There they hid amongst the reeds. They could see a second net being carefully stretched between the other two boats, now also well concealed. Then they waited in silence. After a few minutes Dirk started to ask a question, but was instantly cuffed on the cheek by the headman who growled at him to be silent.

As night fell geese flew low over the reed pool, circled and landed on the water in a flurry of spray. As the birds settled and began to preen their feathers the headman started making a low whooping noise. The punts left the cover of the reeds propelled by hands dipping quietly into the cold water. They crept cautiously towards the birds. The geese were not panicked, but began to swim steadily away from the noise. As the birds sought the sanctuary of the reeds, the headman and the catcher in the other boat drew their net tight, while the punters drove the boats forward towards their waiting companions. The birds at last began to appreciate the danger, but it was too late. The nets were thrown over the squawking mass. Some birds managed to escape through the gaps between the boats, but Conn saw that at least seven geese had been trapped in the mesh. These were carefully untangled and, with feet tied together with twine, left secure on the bottom boards of the punt.

Back at the village there was obvious pleasure at their catch. Dug asked the headman if they could do the same again the next day, but he shook his head. 'If we go out too often the birds will become wise to us and will not return to our pool. If we catch too many now, there will be none for next year. It's the same in the spring. We have to be just as careful when the birds are nesting. We only take one egg from each nest. This way we will have a supply of food not just for now, but for all time.'

The boys left next morning with a fat goose tied at the ankles as a present for Silda. They returned to their oxen and when the tide fell, Huw and Conn finished loading the cart and set off on the return trip to Mai-dun. As the oxen were straining with a full load, Conn suggested they should take an easier track to the top of the Ridgeway where the gradient was not so steep. It was still quite early and they were all optimistic they would get back to Mai-dun before dark.

Julius and Alexis spent the night huddled together with the soldiers in a fold of the land near the summit of the Ridgeway. They felt secure enough to light a fire, but even that flickering warmth could not disguise the winter cold. Julius had talked over with Alexis their commission from Vespasian. He asked his friend to be meticulously careful in drawing any plans for the General. He had already experienced how Vespasian took quick decisions on evidence presented to him. Julius was determined to ensure that his and Alexis's evidence was the best.

During the night they were put on the alert as they tried to sleep by a snorting noise, but it was only a badger who short-sightedly stomped past them, searching for food. In the morning the little party uncurled themselves from where they had been lying and stood to shake the stiffness and cold from their joints. At the top of the ridge they could clearly see the details of Mai-dun with the River Frome in the distance. Behind them they could look back to the bay where the Roman ship was at anchor. Julius had been ordered by Vespasian to select a suitable spot for a signal tower. He found a site that would keep both Mai-dun and the Reed Pool in view and Alexis marked it on his chart, calling it Beacon Hill. Now, if the General decided on a two-pronged attack by sea and by land, the beacon could keep each half informed of the activity of the other.

One of the soldiers pointed out to Julius the considerable activity at Mai-dun. 'Look at the way they're strengthening the fortifications round the western entrance. I think they've heard we're coming.'

Alexis roughly sketched the two horns of the new embankment. 'We must get closer,' he told Julius. 'I need to get some accurate measurements so that our officers can best decide how to attack.'

The group circled widely round the east and north side of the hillfort. Every now and then Alexis would stop to make further drawings and calculations. They had a scare when they were startled by a herd of wild pigs rootling in a birch wood, but they saw no one. From high ground to the west, Alexis completed his sketch of the second gateway and towards dark they made their way back to the comparative safety of the uninhabited Ridgeway.

As they neared the summit they heard whistling and shouting. Julius waved his men down to hide behind some rocks. He told one of the soldiers to go forward to see what was happening. Five minutes later the man returned. 'It's just some kids,' he said. 'They're driving and pulling a couple of miserable looking oxen up the hill with a cartload of stones. These look like possible ammunition for slingshots. They're only youngsters and we can take them easily.'

Julius thought for a moment. 'No,' he said. 'Let them alone. If we kill them all we would do is prevent one load of missiles getting through to the enemy. They could easily get some more. Also, we don't want people to know we've been here.'

The cart reached the top with much cheering from the boys and disappeared down the track that the Romans had just ascended. Julius and his companions pressed on towards the sea and spent a second cold night in the open. In the morning they struck the path Julius and Alexis had used 12 months earlier. The morning mist was lying on the surface of the Reed Pool and the group spread out to try to find a suitable anchorage for ships if Vespasian should decide to use this as his disembarkation point. One of the men called Julius over to a possible landing spot and Julius made him wade out into the freezing channel to show the others how deep the water was. It was an excellent place with gravel instead of mud on the foreshore. Alexis marked his chart accordingly and without further incident they returned to their ship.

Chapter 14
NIGHT RAID

It was now spring and Vespasian and the officers of the Second Cohort sat round a table in the tent that was the General's temporary headquarters. They had reached the Reed Pool near the site selected by Julius, which Vespasian had recently named Clavinium. When Vespasian had returned from the north he had immediately asked to see Julius, and after he had presented his detailed report the summer campaign was planned by the high command. Carinus with the First Cohort and the heavy artillery were to continue to drive forward up the valley of the River Frome while Vespasian and the Second Cohort went by sea. The Roman ships now lay beached in the shelter of the Reed Pool. Clavinium had started to take shape with some basic landing stages and storage huts. The inhabitants of the small fishing village had been cleared out with little resistance and their huts burned down.

On the top of a convenient wooden box the General spread out Alexis's plans and drawings. 'Excellent work,' he told Julius who felt slightly guilty for being praised for something that he could take no credit for. 'This hillfort is our most serious challenge yet, but if we can destroy this Mai-dun, I think there will be little more resistance from the lesser villages. We must be quick and effective. I think the tactics Titus used at Hod should work again here.' His hands moved over the drawings as he explained to his officers how the combination of ballista and onagar had blown away resistance. He even mentioned his own abortive frontal assault. The officers looked surprised and shocked at such a failure by their General, though in fact Vespasian's part in the attack at Hod was known throughout the army.

A messenger knocked on the door post of the tent. 'Signal from Beacon Hill, Sir.'

One of Vespasian's first actions on landing had been to accept the site Julius had selected and to build a beacon on the Ridgeway. This was permanently staffed by four legionaries. Vespasian took the note. 'Good. Carinus and the First Cohort are in sight near the Celtic hillfort. Send a reply that he is to make a secure camp and we will come to join him in 2 days. Tomorrow, gentlemen, we shall go up this Beacon Hill and take a look at the nut we have to crack.'

The arrival of the Roman force by sea had caused considerable excitement in Mai-dun as had the building of the signal tower on the ridge to the south of the settlement. This was almost immediately followed by the news that a second army was advancing by land. The Elders and many of the fighting men met in Bannoc's house realising that the hard work of the winter months was now to be tested. Spies reported that the land army consisted of over 400 soldiers and that these were supported by nearly 30 carts carrying supplies and the artillery that had been much discussed by the military leaders of Mai-dun. The catapults that had destroyed the gates at Hod were Bannoc's biggest worry. Would the new ramparts be strong enough to keep the gates intact under the expected hail of rocks?

The discussion was leading nowhere when Rolf made a suggestion. 'We know the baggage carts, including the artillery, are travelling more slowly than the fighting soldiers. I expect these will spend the night at the river crossing 5 miles behind where the main army is camped. Why don't we send a raiding party to destroy these fearsome weapons we have heard about? Without them I doubt if the Roman attack can succeed.'

The plan was discussed with enthusiasm until Garth pointed out that all it needed was for the army by the sea to be alerted and the raiding party would be cut off from returning to Mai-dun. Rolf thought for a while and then spoke forcefully. 'The soldiers in the signal tower on the ridge are in a key position to let that army know what we are up to. But if we also destroy the tower at the same time as we attack the rock hurlers, the army on the beach will not be aware of what we are up to. We will be safely back behind our walls before they can get their reinforcements together.'

The warriors who were fed up with passively waiting to be attacked, enthusiastically accepted the plan. Rolf volunteered to lead the raid and he asked that his son Huw should be responsible for the destruction of the tower. Bannoc questioned whether Huw, at 16, was not a little young for such responsibility, but Rolf reminded him that the two of them had led similar raids on local tribes in Gaul when they were much the same age. Bannoc approved the attack.

Rolf went home to tell his son of the plan and to brief him as to what was expected. 'It is important that the tower is put out of action before our raid starts. You must attack as soon as it gets dark. There are reported to be four soldiers in the tower, so take a group of six men. There must be no chance of anyone escaping and the tower must be destroyed. You mustn't use fire as that would alert those by the sea.'

Conn pleaded with his friend to be included in this adventure and Huw agreed, 'But remember, you are under my orders. I will also ask Ox, Serap, Rodden and Bran to come too.' They set out to find their companions.

Ox's real name was Brendan, but everyone called him Ox. He was a large and amiable young man who quickly agreed to come. Serap's father had been one of the Council of Elders. When he was killed Bannoc had adopted the young boy into his house. Serap knew about the trip from Bannoc and was enthusiastically ready to leave. Rodden was newly married to Alaynor who was expecting a baby. He was not sure if being married agreed with him, and was quite ready to escape the confines of his small hut. Conn did not know Bran as well as he knew the other three, but the boy was keen enough and Huw assured him Bran would not let them down.

Both raiding parties, heavily armed with spears, slings and daggers, left by the eastern gate at the same time. Rolf wished his son good luck. The young men knew the paths well and had no difficulty finding their route, as it was still some time before dark. They slipped through the yellow furze bushes, using them as cover, and arrived on top of the ridge close to the signal tower well. It was not really a tower, but rather a platform about four paces square on stilts about the height of a man. A notched log lay against one side to provide a rough ladder for the men to climb up. The beacon fire, with a supply of logs ready, was a few paces away. Huw could see one man on watch up on the platform and could hear a murmur of voices from the little campsite under the shelter. Smoke from a fire, conversation and occasional laughter suggested that two or three men were off duty at ground level.

Huw had already outlined his plan to his companions and waved them forward. Serap, Bran and Ox moved down the northern slope of the hill while Conn, who to his disgust was not allowed to be part of the attack, slithered down the other side. Conn's responsibility was to make sure that none of the Romans escaped towards the sea. Leaving Ox to do the same job on the northern slope, Serap and Bran approached the tower from the opposite side to Huw, deliberately making a considerable noise. Three of the Romans, suspicious at the row, came out of their little camp to see what was going on. They relaxed when they saw the two apparently harmless young men approaching and one of them called out. What they did not see was Huw and Rodden creeping up behind them. A quick slash from Huw's dagger and the first guard was dead with a slit throat. Serap and Bran rushed the other two. One was bundled to the ground and angry knives slashed through the leather jerkin until he was dead.

The survivor of this brutal attack managed to draw his short sword and hacked at Bran, wounding him in the head. He then dashed for the ladder and took refuge with his companion up on the platform. While they were up there they were comparatively safe from their attackers. One of them, realising help could still be summoned from the camp by the sea, stood up with his signalling flags. He raised the flags above his head, but with a twirl from Huw's sling, a deadly stone caught him on the temple. He fell and rolled off the edge to the ground where he was quickly butchered.

The last of the guards lay low on the platform and waited. While Serap looked at Bran's wound, Huw and Rodden began to saw through the cords that bound the planks to the stilts. The first rope parted and the platform sagged a little. It would not take long for the whole lot to come down. The last Roman soldier realised that if he remained where he was his position would become hopeless. He crawled to the edge of the tower and jumped. He landed in some bushes, rolled, scrambled to his feet and started running down hill. Huw shouted a warning to Conn who had been watching the events up the hill. The panic-stricken guard saw Conn at the last minute and swerved towards him. Both were armed with spears, but one was a novice and the other a long-serving warrior. No doubt if the guard had managed to calm himself, as an experienced fighter he would have had no problem in dealing with a 15-year-old boy, but the brutal dispatch of his companions had unsettled him. He ran at Conn with his spear levelled at the heart. At the last moment Conn dropped to his knees and dug the butt of his spear into the ground. The Roman's spear caught Conn high on his shoulder, but not before the soldier's running impetus had impaled him on Conn's crude weapon.

When Huw and Rodden rushed down to them, both bodies were lying in a tangle. Conn's wound was bleeding profusely and he was groaning with pain. The Roman was dead. Rodden pulled the legionary's body off Conn and Huw knelt down to comfort his friend. Both boys were scared by what had just happened, but gradually realised that any danger was over. Huw gently pulled out the Roman spear from Conn's shoulder and used his dagger to cut a piece of cloth from the dead soldier's tunic to make a pad to cover Conn's wound. Rodden helped the two boys to their feet and, shaken but elated, they walked back to the tower.

There they found Ox and Serap kneeling over the wounded Bran. The boy had a deep gash in his skull and was quietly whimpering. None of them knew how to deal with such an injury, but it was obvious that Bran was not going to be walking back to Mai-dun. They decided to complete their mission by destroying the tower first, and then with bits of wood they built a sledge on which they carefully laid Bran, who was by now unconscious.

Before they set off Huw said to the others, 'When my father returns from a raid he always brings back trophies as proof of his success. I suggest we take some things from these Romans.' They collected swords, daggers and cloaks from the corpses and stacked them around Bran on the sledge. Finally, as was the way with Celts, they cut off the heads of the dead soldiers and added them to their heap of spoils.

Conn, though feeling faint, had managed with help from the others to walk down the hill. It was 2 hours before the sorry group arrived back in Mai-dun. The sword slash had gone right through Bran's skull and on the journey home he died. Ox had taken responsibility for the sledge and insisted on dragging the body back so that Bran's family could give him the full funeral rights. When they entered the settlement he volunteered to carry the body to Bran's hut.

Huw helped Conn stagger into Rolf's hut where Morwen and the twins were attempting to sleep in their places on the floor. Silda, who was waiting for her husband and her son to return, was fussing around the fire. Morwen let out a cry when she saw both boys covered in Conn's blood and rushed towards them, but Silda, who was used to dealing with wounds, pushed her daughter aside. She quickly discovered that Huw was uninjured and that Conn would recover when his wound had been dealt with. As before, Morwen was sent to fetch Maddoc. Silda sat Conn on the floor and taking off his shirt started to clean round the shoulder. Huw began to tell his mother all that had happened, but she had little time for chatting.

'As commander of the expedition you shouldn't leave it to Serap to report to Bannoc. Go and do it yourself,' and she pushed him out of the hut.

By the time Maddoc arrived Conn was lying down and the bleeding had largely stopped. The old man moved Conn's arm up and down which made the boy wince with pain and the bleeding start again. He prodded and poked at the wound and told Silda that he had probably damaged a muscle, but should quickly recover. He cleaned the wound with cold water and then from his basket brought out a precious handful of sphagnum moss. He placed this over the injury and held it in place with an old piece of cloth. Once again he produced his little jar of poppy juice and Conn soon fell asleep exhausted. Silda asked Morwen to sit by the sleeping youth, which she did gladly. Occasionally she stroked his head, but of this Conn was unaware.

Just after dawn Rolf's party returned triumphant. Three men had been killed in the initial assault, but they had found the baggage carts weakly guarded and had set fire to everything including four giant catapults. They had seen warning fires being lit to alert the guards on Beacon Hill, but no answering flames from the ridge suggeseted that Huw's party had been successful. The gates were shut and the Celts celebrated.

In the morning Vespasian, accompanied by Julius, his bodyguards Novak and Goran and a small force of legionaries, rode up to Beacon Hill. They were still a mile away when the General noticed the ruins of the tower, so on getting to the top he was not surprised to find the soldiers' bodies. He cursed himself for leaving such a small force alone in enemy territory and cursed the enemy for their savagery. He swore that the butchered soldiers would be avenged. Julius pointed out the columns of smoke at the Frome crossing and Vespasian realised that there would be more bad news that day. He looked towards Mai-dun. Alexis's drawings had given him a good idea of what to expect, but he looked grim when for the first time he saw the impressive fortress.

He spoke to one of the soldiers. 'Go back to camp and tell the senior centurion what has happened here. Tell him to recover these bodies and to give them the proper rites. We will go on and meet Carinus and find out what has been happening to him.'

Chapter 15
THE FIRST ASSAULT

Vespasian and Carinus stood in silence gazing at the smoking ruins of the baggage carts. Carinus was the first to speak, making his report to the General. 'Both onagars are completely ruined. The artillery-men tell me that we do not have sufficient quality wood to make the repairs. I will have to send to Lake Camp asking Maximus for replacements. Six of the ballistas are damaged, but the engineers think they can be repaired by tomorrow. Three legionaries were killed by the Celts and four others wounded. Sixteen of the auxiliaries who were looking after the supplies were killed as well. It was a well-executed attack, swift and ruthless. They seemed to know what they were aiming for.'

He paused and waited for Vespasian to speak. When the General remained silent Carinus continued. 'I miscalculated badly, General. I did not think the enemy would risk coming out from behind their walls and I had failed to double the guards, as is your standing orders when enemies are near. We sent reinforcements down here from the legionary camp immediately they signalled they were under attack, but by the time these arrived the damage had been done and the enemy had fled. I'm sorry I failed you, Sir.'

'Yes indeed, Carinus, you have failed, but so have I.' He told Carinus about the attack on Beacon Hill and the massacre of the soldiers there. 'I too did not anticipate that the Celts would go on the offensive. We have all become over-confident with our successes and the result of this is 23 men dead, a number we can ill afford to lose. Clear up this mess here and bring the remainder of the baggage train up to the legionary camp. Send a messenger to the Second Cohort by the sea and tell them to march to join us this afternoon. I will go and have a closer look at this Mai-dun and the butchers who live in it.'

'Now we know they are prepared to attack, take care, Sir,' said Carinus.

'I will,' Vespasian answered. 'But with these two to look after me,' he indicated Novak and Goran, 'I'll be safe enough. We meet again at the camp this evening at the sixth hour.'

By evening there were 600 Roman soldiers camped 2 miles to the north of Mai-dun. Vespasian outlined his plan to Carinus and Julius. 'Without the onagers we cannot hope to assault the gates. I know from our attack on Hod that we will suffer too many casualties. The legion is already under-strength and I want to remove this obstacle,' he waved an arm towards Mai-dun, 'but losing as few men as possible in the process. We will change our tactics for we have here a thinking enemy. Tomorrow we will advance with two full centuries stretched in line all along this north side of the fortress. They will take their battle shields with them and move forward behind these. When they reach the top of the first rampart they will be under fire from enemy slingers, but they should be safe as long as they hold their shields high. Any soldier who is injured is to be brought back here and his place in the line immediately filled. The job of this first wave is to remove any debris from the top of the first barrier. I have seen thorn bushes, stakes and other obstacles there. All these are to be taken away down the hill towards us. There is no hurry, but the rampart must be thoroughly cleared.

When it is, the signal for withdrawal will be sounded. The men will fall back and a second line made up of the Third and Fourth Centuries will take their place. They will go down into the ditch carrying ladders with them. These they will use to go up the other side to clean out the second rampart in the same way. You, Carinus, will place all our ballistas that can be made to work along the first wall, which we will have just cleared, and shoot at any of their slingers who show themselves. This way we can give our men covering fire.

When the second rampart is cleared the signal for withdrawal will again be sounded. The ballistas will continue to cover our soldiers as they pull back. By that time the defenders will be exhausted, and fresh legionaries should have little problem. The shields must at all times make a solid line – any break and their slingers will have a target. Carinus, make sure the men understand that we will withdraw twice. There is no golden crown for being the first over the wall tomorrow. Are there any questions?'

'Sir, I would like to lead my men into battle. Do I have your permission?' Carinus asked.

Vespasian was on the point of refusing, but he understood that Carinus needed a successful action to make up for his error that had cost them the baggage train. Perhaps too he remembered a similar request he had made to his brother, Titus, at Hod.

'All right, Marcus Carinus. You will command from the centre of the line. However, I will send Novak and Goran with you with clear instructions to make sure you are safe at all times. I need you uninjured. We march forward tomorrow morning immediately after the men have breakfasted.'

The weather worsened during the night and it was raining steadily when Carinus surveyed his attacking force next morning. One hundred and sixty men stretched along the north side of the hillfort, armed with short swords and defended by their long battle shields. They were still outside the effective range of the enemy's missiles while Carinus explained to the officers the General's orders. He then told the trumpeter to sound the advance.

The attack went as Vespasian had planned except it took much longer than he had anticipated for his soldiers to clear the rampart. The Celts had sunk long wooden stakes into the ground supported by large boulders and the Romans worked slowly to clear these away, making sure they were protected from the hail of missiles by a wall of shields. Piece by piece the intricate defences it had taken the Celts all winter to construct were dismantled.

It was slow work and it was the middle of the afternoon before Carinus was satisfied that the first wall was clear. Now, he reckoned, was time for some offensive action. First he sent for the two specialists on the *scorpion* under his command. Vespasian had ordered that each century was to have at least one soldier who could handle the giant crossbow, which in the hands of an expert was pin-point accurate up to 100 paces. The two arrived carrying their weapons and saluted Carinus.

'I need some of these barbarians dead before night-fall. There's a big fellow with yellow hair walking arrogantly along the walls, looks like one of their officers. Spread yourselves out, select a target and see what you can bag. Watch out for our ballistas as I am going to order them up now.' He immediately called for the ballistas to be set up at intervals along the parapet and they quickly found their range.

A shower of metal bolts began to slam into the woodwork where the Celts were standing. Up to that moment they had felt completely safe behind their wall. Now for the first time they had to duck down for safety. Carinus knew that, in the wet, the leather coils of the ballistas would soon lose their elasticity, but he reckoned his men needed to vent some Roman aggression before they went back to camp.

After a while he sent a runner down to Vespasian who, no doubt impatiently, was waiting below with the third and fourth centuries. The general decided there was insufficient time that day to start on the second line of defence and moved his men back to the camp. Carinus ordered the withdrawal to be sounded.

Bannoc and Garth had expected a Roman attack, but they had little idea where it would be delivered. Garth was confident that the gates were well defended, and he was determined to move his fighters around the perimeter to meet an assault from whichever direction it came.

Early in the morning, Conn, his shoulder heavily bandaged, took his position with Huw on one of the central slingers' platforms on the northern wall. Some small boys, Dirk and Dug amongst them, kept the slingers supplied with stones. They scurried with basket-loads of pebbles between the ammunition pits and inner palisade and defence platforms, urged on by Rolf. As the sun rose Rolf went round the whole perimeter to make sure his men understood what was required. The slowly advancing line of shields surprised the defenders who had been anticipating an all-out assault. They shouted abuse, slung stones and cheered when a Roman shield was hit, though they realised the range was too great for them to inflict any real damage. Much to his irritation Conn found that he could not use his sling because of his wound, but he stood next to his friend, encouraging him.

Nothing much seemed to happen all day and by mid-afternoon both boys were getting bored. Conn was leaning on the wooden palisade watching the Romans at work when he felt an iron bolt slam into one of the wooden uprights near his head. He ducked down shaking with shock. His shoulder ached and he sat down on the floor boarding trying to regain his composure. Huw joined him, crouching. 'Are you alright?' he asked. Conn nodded and Huw passed him a flask of water.

'Thanks,' Conn muttered, drinking thirstily. 'This is not what I expected at all. Why don't they attack us properly? I don't think we've managed to kill any of their soldiers yet.'

'I think one of our slingers on the next platform has just been shot,' Huw said, peering through the planking. As Conn shuffled over to take a look, they heard the Roman trumpeter sound the withdrawal. Both boys cautiously edged forward on hands and knees to see what was happening. Conn stood up and shouted excitedly, pointing at the retreating Romans. Huw joined him to see what his friend was looking at when a metal bolt thudded into the middle of his stomach. His whole body arched backwards and then slipped sideways and over the edge of the wooden defences. Conn, shocked, watched Huw topple into the ditch.

Ignoring the pain in his shoulder, Conn leaped to the edge of the platform and began to climb down. Others tried to hold him back, but he shook himself free and scrambled and scraped down the wall until his feet landed on the grass. He was now shielded from the enemy by the second rampart as he ran forward to Huw's body. Huw lay crumpled on his side with the wooden shaft of the bolt obscenely sticking out from his shirt, now covered in blood. Conn gently turned his friend onto his back. It was obvious that he was dead. Shocked, he knelt beside Huw's body wondering what to do next, but then realised there was nothing he could do. He put his head in his hands and sobbed.

A while later Conn heard others coming to join him. Rolf

was there beside him and together they carried Huw along the ditch and in through the east gate. Conn could hear Silda and Morwen keening their grief as they approached the hut. The group of men escorting the body helped them lay their sad burden down outside and the two women came out. Silda threw herself on to her son's body. Conn stood numb with grief.

Bannoc ordered that those killed that day and those killed in the two raids should be buried with ceremony by nightfall. Maddoc chose a spot for the graves by the eastern gate as near to the rising sun as possible. As the battle would be resumed next morning there was not time for a full Celtic burial, normally a 3-day ritual, so Maddoc conducted a ceremony in accordance with Druidical rites. Several forlorn groups assembled round the newly dug pits just before sundown. Huw and Bran were buried together in one grave so that they could remain friends in the afterlife. Rolf had not been able to remove the metal bolt from his son's body, so he left it there, covering the wound discreetly with the boy's cloak. It was normal to provide the dead with food on their journey to the afterlife so Silda placed a leg of lamb between the bodies of Huw and Bran and some of her son's favourite cooked dishes. Rolf knelt down and carefully laid Huw's sword and his own bronze ring next to the boy. Conn held Morwen's hand as she came forward and added a valuable brooch her father had given her. Conn had no doubt what he wanted to give Huw. Earlier he had collected from Maddoc's house the little Samian bowl Julius had given him. He leant over the grave and laid his only possession of value next to his friend. Dirk and Dug were, for once, shocked into silence. As the men pushed the earth back into the graves it started to rain gently. Maddoc walked round the grave-site chanting and swinging his incense dish with burning pine resin. The families wept quietly as the pungent smoke rose into the night sky.

Conn felt that Rolf and Silda would want to be left alone that evening, but as he turned to go to his own hut Rolf beckoned. 'They will come again tomorrow, Conn, and if necessary the day after and the day after that. They will not give up until they have conquered us. Morwen told me of Maddoc's dream, the one that foretold the destruction of Mai-dun. I have talked with him and he believes that, even though the village will be cold and empty, the people will be saved. I don't know how this will be.'

He paused and laid his hand on Conn's shoulder. 'Now Huw is dead, I trust that you will look after Morwen.'

Conn protested that he would look after all the family, but Rolf shook his head.

'You don't understand what I mean, son. I entrust Morwen to your special care. Look after her well.'

Chapter 16
CAPTURE

It was still raining next morning when Vespasian came to join Carinus who was standing outside his tent looking across the drab landscape to Mai-dun. 'What are you thinking about, Marcus?'

Carinus was touched that the General should use his personal name instead of the more formal name by which he was known in the army. 'I was thinking of my farm in Lusitania and of Romana, my wife.'

'Do you have children?' Vespasian asked.

'I have a son Rufinus and a daughter Carina. Rufinus will be 8 now, but I have not seen either of them for 3 years.' The two men fell silent and Vespasian thought of his own family in Rome growing up without him.

'When were you given your farm?' Vespasian continued.

'Oh, it was about 6 years ago when the legion was stationed in Lusitania. Caligula was Emperor and he needed to keep the army sweet so we were all given small plots of land. I grow grapes and make some wine, but we will never grow rich from it. At least the sun shines in summer there.'

'There's a good reason why Romans call this the misty isle,' Vespasian laughed. 'By the gods, I could do with some sunshine to finish this lot off. What did you think about today's attack plan?' he asked abruptly.

Carinus considered carefully before he answered. He didn't want Vespasian to think he was over-cautious because he knew that caution was not a quality the General valued, but he needed to give an honest opinion. 'The men of the Second Legion are tough enough to fight in any weather, and I have no doubt that if you give the order we can capture the fort before nightfall. We will not be able to use our ballistas today because of the rain, and so the defenders will be that much safer behind their parapets. We should have no difficulty clearing the second rampart because we have plenty of ladders, even though the ground will be slippery. However, if it was my decision I should leave the final assault until tomorrow when I hope it will be drier.'

Although Vespasian was anxious to press on with the destruction of Mai-dun and to avenge the slaughtered guards he appreciated Carinus's thoughtful words. 'I agree. Tell the men that our objective today is solely to clear the second rampart. We attack the walls tomorrow.'

With the plan decided Vespasian seemed to relax. 'What were the injury figures from yesterday?' he asked.

Carinus drew a list out of his pocket. 'One broken ankle, I believe he put his foot down a rabbit hole; two men out of action through head wounds, but the surgeon expects them to be fighting tomorrow; apart from that, several bruises, but nothing serious. We will have to be careful today as we will be working much closer to the enemy.'

'We have plenty of time today. I don't want any unnecessary heroics.' Vespasian looked pleased at such a light casualty list.

That morning the men worked steadily on the second rampart behind their shield wall. The wooden posts were sunk deep into the chalk and it was a slow business digging them out. The damp weather had made the ballistas and *scorpions* ineffective, and the Celts, unhindered by the terrible bolts, fired their own missiles at the Romans, but caused few injuries. Most problems were the result of the slipperiness of the wet chalk. Carinus walked up and down the line accompanied by Novak and Goran who protected him with their shields. The rain came down even heavier and swept across the top of Mai-dun, soaking both defenders and attackers.

By mid-morning Carinus, who was inspecting progress at the eastern end of the line, decided that the rampart was sufficiently clear for an attack next day and ordered the signaller to sound the withdrawal. As he did so, Novak, who was using his shield to cover Carinus, was hit in the throat by a well-aimed flying stone. He fell to the ground making a horrible gurgling sound. Carinus seized the shield which Novak had dropped and covered his stricken bodyguard with it.

'Goran, and you, soldier,' he shouted to the next shield in line, 'take this man back to the infirmary, fast. We are all returning to camp now. I don't need you here any longer.' The two of them rolled Novak onto one of the long shields and slid him down into the ditch. From where he was standing on the rampart Carinus could just make them out as they picked the shield up and joined the column returning to quarters.

Mai-dun was by now almost entirely hidden by the rain, which was falling increasingly heavily. *I'm glad we're not trying to go over the wall in this weather,* Carinus thought to himself. He looked round and turned to follow his retiring soldiers, but as he did so his leather sandal skidded on the exposed chalk made slippery by the rain. He fell backwards and lost control. His body rolled and bounced 30 ft down the steep bank into the ditch beneath the final rampart. He lay still.

Conn was standing miserably on the wooden walkway near the east gate. He was wet through and this day his wound ached, though not half as much as his heart ached

119

for his dead friend. As he couldn't use his sling, Rolf had ordered him to take a turn at keeping watch now the enemy had pulled back. He was pleased when Morwen climbed the ladder to join him. She stretched her cloak over his shoulders and they stood in comfortable silence. Conn was thinking how he and Huw would never again go fishing. Morwen too was remembering her brother, but she was also thinking how safe she felt with Conn under her cloak.

The rain was slanting across the platform when Morwen urgently whispered, 'What was that noise?' Conn had heard nothing. 'There it is again, from down in the ditch.' This time Conn did hear a faint cry. The two of them concentrated hard against the drumming rain and again both heard the sound, like that of an animal in pain. 'Shall I go and tell my father?'

Conn thought about it. Properly he should have let Rolf know immediately, but deep inside he felt that this was something he had to do by himself. The sound might be nothing at all, but he had a premonition that this was going to be important to him and to Mai-dun. 'I'm going to take a look. You stay on watch here and I'll find out what's making the noise. I'll be back before anyone's missed me.' Morwen protested, but Conn was determined. He cautiously lowered himself over the edge of the platform with much more care than he had the day before. Easing himself down one of the posts he reached the grass and slithered and slid to the floor of the ditch. He moved forward towards where he thought the noise had come from.

Carinus lay sprawled across the bottom of the ditch. As his falling body had careered to the foot of the slope his flailing arm had become impaled on one of the sharpened stakes, which the Celts had placed there to slow down an assault. The point of the stake had pierced through his wrist, breaking one of the bones, and had transfixing him where he lay. The shock of the pain had made him pass out. What

Conn and Morwen had heard was Carinus returning to consciousness. Conn edged towards the groaning Roman. When he saw the sharp point of the wood thrusting through the man's wrist he realised immediately that he was no danger to him. He drew his dagger. One stab into the throat of the helpless man and he could have a trophy to take back. 'It's all right, Morwen,' he called back to her. 'It's a dying Roman.'

Carinus opened his eyes when he heard the voice. He could not understand what was said, but he recognised what the dagger meant and for just a moment he felt a flicker of fear deep inside before his eyes closed again. Conn was reminded of a similar look from the fawn lying helpless in the alder bush and remembered Morwen's words at that time. This was no monster. Though an enemy he was also a human being. He thought back to Huw's death yesterday and how useless he had been to help then. Perhaps this time he could do something. He put his dagger back in its sheath and seeing a leather bottle lying strapped to Carinus's waist he picked it up and unstoppered it. He held the neck of the bottle to the man's lips and gently poured some of the wine into his mouth. Carinus groaned and his eyes fluttered open again.

He said something in a language Conn did not understand. 'I'm going to help you,' Conn replied, although he was aware that his words meant nothing to the injured Roman. He realised that if he tried to pull the stick from the man's wrist either the shock would kill him or he would bleed to death. He continued to speak to him in the Celtic language as he again drew his dagger and started to whittle away at the stake where it had entered the shattered wrist. Carinus groaned with pain every time there was any movement, but by now he understood that Conn was trying to help him.

After minutes of sawing Conn managed to cut through the wood and free Carinus. The boy cut away a strip of his own shirt and fashioned a crude sling and secured Carinus's arm to his body. He then helped him to his feet. Carinus staggered and leaned on Conn. The boy was confused and did not know what to do next. If he took the injured Roman back to Mai-dun, he would certainly be put to death. That did not seem right. He decided to help him back over the ramparts and leave him free to find his own way back to the Roman camp.

Vespasian was the first to realise that Carinus had not returned. He summoned Goran and asked for an explanation. This, of course, Goran could not give. Biting back his anger, Vespasian quickly organised a search party and told Goran to lead the group back to where he had last seen the man he was supposed to be protecting. The rescue party, led by a centurion and directed by Goran, found their way to the top of the now abandoned outer rampart. Through the rain the centurion could see two figures painfully struggling up the grassy slope towards them. 'Look there,' he shouted. Goran drew his sword and rushed down to meet them. Conn would have been instantly skewered, but Carinus threw himself in front of the boy, quickly explaining that Conn was his rescuer, and together they helped the rapidly weakening officer up to where the rest of the patrol waited. Carinus gave further explanation to the centurion before his legs gave way completely. Conn was now a prisoner. His hands were secured behind him and the little group made their way back to the Roman camp.

Vespasian came to visit Carinus in the hospital tent as soon as the surgeons had finished with him. The tent had been prepared to receive many casualties but was empty apart from Carinus, the legionary who had broken his ankle and Novak who was unconscious in a corner. The doctors, hovering round Carinus's bed, were ordered away by Vespasian. 'How are you feeling, my friend?' he asked.

Carinus was still in considerable pain, but he was

grateful that the General had taken the time to come and see him. 'It hurts like Hades, but the doctor says I'll live. He's not certain if he can save my hand yet.' He explained the circumstances of how he had come to fall and added, 'Don't be hard on Goran. He was only carrying out my orders.'

Vespasian said nothing, conscious that he had just given the bodyguard a savage tongue lashing, but privately deciding to take him off the 2 weeks' latrine duty that had been his punishment.

'How is the boy?' Carinus asked.

'What boy?' Vespasian had heard nothing of Conn's capture.

'The boy who spared my life. Without his care and courage I would certainly be dead.' He told Vespasian how he had come round, aware that he could not move, to see a boy bending over him, and how this boy had sawed through the stake and helped him to safety. 'I would like to see him to thank him.'

Vespasian assured him he would find out what had happened. As soon as he left the tent, he sought Julius and told him to find the prisoner and take him to see Carinus. Julius learned that Conn was tied up in the baggage park and discovered the boy sheltering from rain under one of the wagons. He told the guard to release him on the General's orders. The man did so and dragged him out by his leg.

Julius did not recognise the bedraggled figure as the boy he had met one December morning 18 months previously, but Conn immediately remembered him. 'You're the one who gave me the bowl; you told me you were a trader.' He struggled to escape from the guard, but the soldier had a firm grip on his arm and Conn had to be content with once again spitting at Julius. Julius, uncomfortably aware of the lies he had told that day, said nothing, but led Conn to the hospital.

Conn was amazed at the amount of space and how clean everything was in the tent. Julius took him over to the bed and Carinus held out his uninjured hand and gripped Conn's arm. Conn winced with pain, as his own wound was still raw. Carinus noticed this and called the surgeon over to examine the shoulder. The legion's doctor had considerable experience in dealing with battle injuries and he studied the wound with interest. 'It's a spear thrust. I don't know what this muck is that's covering the hole, but it seems to be keeping it clean. There doesn't seem to be any infection. The boy's lucky. I think he has been well cared for and should get better without my help.' He called for a clean bandage and rebound the shoulder after carefully repacking the wound with the moss and chickweed Maddoc had put there 3 days earlier.

Carinus turned to Conn and asked Julius to translate for him. 'Thank you for saving my life. I am sorry your help to me has made you a prisoner.' Conn said nothing so Carinus went on, 'Why did you not kill me when you had the chance?'

Conn remained silent and Julius, who thought he had not understood, repeated the question. 'I understand,' Conn said angrily, because he had not yet forgiven Julius for what he thought was a betrayal. Then he started to speak to Carinus, slowly at first and then with growing confidence. He told them what Morwen had said to him when they had discovered the fawn by the stream. 'When I was with the raiding party we killed the soldiers at the watchtower, but it didn't feel right when we cut off their heads. War is not the game I expected it to be.' Julius had to ask him to slow down so that he could keep up with the translation for Carinus.

'Yesterday my friend was killed and last night we buried him. I don't understand why he had to die. When I found you lying in the same place as Huw, you were unconscious. I could have killed you at that moment. Then you woke up.

Though it did not show on your face I knew you had fear in your heart. I saw you as a man and not as an enemy. I did not see why you had to die.'

He went on, 'Rolf says you will defeat us either tomorrow or the next day and we will probably all be killed. Why should this be? We have not harmed you in any way. All we want to do is to live our lives.'

Carinus said to Julius, 'Ask him if there are others in the hillfort who think like him.'

'Some of the Council I expect want to fight on, but not the people. I know the Teacher doesn't like fighting and I think Rolf, one of our Elders, has had enough,' Conn admitted.

Carinus and Julius discussed Conn's answers and both agreed this was important information Vespasian should know. 'Leave the boy with me, I'll take responsibility for him,' Carinus said. 'Also ask the General if he will come back here.'

Half an hour later, when Vespasian and Julius came to the bedside, Conn was eating a bowl of porridge with fingers that were not very clean. He wiped his hand on his shirt and set the bowl down on the floor. Julius spoke to the General. 'This boy is called Conn. He is the one who initially gave me all the information about Mai-dun 18 months ago. He doesn't like me very much because he thinks I betrayed his trust.' Julius looked saddened. 'He is right in that.'

Vespasian snorted. 'Rubbish. You did what you were told to do. What has this boy to tell us?' Conn was asked to repeat his comments to the General. 'Ask him if he thinks they will surrender without fighting.'

'Only if they think they will be safe. No one wants to die,' Conn answered.

Vespasian thought a while. 'I can promise safety to everyone except those who butchered my guards.' Julius translated the General's offer to Conn and the two of them had a heated conversation, which the two senior officers listened to but could not understand. 'What's he saying, Tribune? Tell me,' said Vespasian impatiently.

Julius again spoke to Conn who nodded in agreement before he turned to Vespasian. 'He thinks if you offer them life the people will want to give up without more fighting, but Bannoc, the Chief, will be difficult to persuade. The boy has asked me to tell you that he was one of those who took part in the raid on Beacon Hill.'

Vespasian looked grim. 'Ask him why they cut the heads off my soldiers.'

Conn's answer was long and Julius struggled to translate. 'It is their custom. No disrespect is intended to brave enemies. By bringing trophy heads back from battle, warriors hope to take for themselves some of the courage from those they have killed. Two of his friends who were on the raid are already dead; one of them was the leader. Conn does not feel that anything was gained from their action.' Julius stopped speaking and there was silence in the tent. Then he continued. 'He was injured and I don't think he actually took part in mutilating the bodies, but he refuses to distance himself from the action. I tried to persuade him not to tell you of the part he played, but he insisted that you should know.' He went on quietly, 'Perhaps he has acquired some of the courage of a Roman.'

'He's a deep one, that boy,' Carinus butted in. 'He said he knew I was scared, which I was because I thought the little swine was going to cut my throat, but I swear that not a flicker of fear crossed my face. It was as if he could see inside me.'

Vespasian locked his fingers together in front of him and paced up and down in the tent, deep in thought. There was silence for some minutes. 'Tell him he has spoken well,' he said at last to Julius. 'Tomorrow I shall need him again.'

Chapter 17
NEGOTIATIONS

Conn, wearing a dark red legionary's short cloak, stood with Julius outside the eastern gate of Mai-dun. They were accompanied by 50 soldiers of the Third Cohort and sensibly remained just outside missile range. It was an hour before midday.

Conn had spent the previous night tied up underneath the baggage cart under guard. The different sounds of a legionary marching camp made sleep difficult for him, but eventually he had drifted off. At first light his guard had woken him and taken him to the hospital tent to see Carinus. He had made a formal speech of thanks in Latin which Conn could not understand and presented him with a cloak which the guard had helped him pin on correctly. One of the General's orderlies then accompanied Conn outside. Vespasian had assembled 200 battle-hardened veterans in full uniform. For 30 minutes the centurions drilled them with marching, counter marching and swordplay. The display had finished with the whole cohort advancing in triple line towards their commander, rhythmically banging the handles of their short swords on their shields. Ten paces from Vespasian, on command, the line stopped and the legion saluted. The show was designed to impress Conn, and the boy was awestruck with what he had seen. In his mind he compared the fighting professionalism of the Romans with his own companions' enthusiasm. Inexperienced though he was, he realised that enthusiasm and raw courage alone would not be enough to defeat Roman training and discipline.

As one of the few Romans who could speak the Celtic language, Julius was given an important commission by Vespasian, and so he arrived at the eastern gate of Mai-dun accompanied by Conn. The boy called out to the gateman and Bannoc himself appeared on the watchtower. Conn asked if his companion, Julius, could enter in safety to have talks with the leaders. Bannoc had a brief discussion with Rolf and Garth who were with him on the tower and then agreed. Conn and Julius walked forward to the great gates, leaving their guard behind. Julius, remembering the fate of the watchmen on Beacon Hill, felt very vulnerable as he waited for them to open, but Conn had explained to him that the idea of a messenger approaching under safe conduct was not unknown to the Celts. Eventually one of the gates half opened and the two of them went in to Mai-dun.

All morning the defenders on the walls had been waiting, expecting an assault. These men now left their positions and drifted towards the eastern entrance to see what was happening. Conn and Julius were faced with a large crowd, all chattering and calling out to them. Conn's cloak was much commented on, and when he saw Morwen and her mother in the crowd he risked a small wave. Nervously he led Julius towards Bannoc who had taken up position near the spot where Huw and the others had been buried 2 days earlier. Bannoc formally greeted Julius. His reply in the Celtic language produced a murmur of appreciation from those who heard it. Bannoc with Rolf and Garth led the way to the Chieftain's hut where Maddoc was already seated waiting for them. The councillors sat in a circle around the hearth on one side with Conn and Julius seated on the other. Conn spoke first, telling the leaders how he had rescued Carinus the previous day. This they already knew from Rolf as Morwen had told her father the little that she had managed to see through the rain. The boy went on to tell them about his meeting with Vespasian and finished with a description of the display of military power that had so impressed him earlier. The Elders talked quietly among themselves and then Bannoc invited Julius to speak.

The young tribune had been well briefed by Vespasian in what he should say. He stood up. 'I have come with the authority of my general, Titus Flavius Vespasianus, who sends his greetings to the leaders of Mai-dun. He has orders from the Emperor in Rome to conquer all the land of the *Atrebates*, the *Durotriges* and the *Dumnonii*. He has already captured 20 hillforts including those at Hod and White Rings as well as the trading post at Hengistbury. Mai-dun will be next. When the defenders of these forts have surrendered without a fight, they have been allowed to live in peace. Where there has been fighting, the leaders and the people have had to pay with their lives. Tomorrow the Roman army will occupy Mai-dun. Do not doubt this. What Conn has told you about our soldiers is true. If you oppose our general, tomorrow most of your people and all the leaders will die. If you agree to surrender some will be taken to Rome as slaves, but it is not necessary that anyone should be killed. Vespasian invites you, Bannoc, and the one who is called the Teacher to come and hear this from his own lips. He will guarantee, in honour, that both of you will be returned here safely. I will go outside now so that you can discuss this in private and talk further with Conn.' With that, Julius left the hut.

Bannoc turned to Conn. 'Tell me about their army,' he demanded. Conn described that morning's military manoeuvres in dramatic detail and it was obvious to all of them that he was stunned by what he had seen. Bannoc continued, 'Do you think we can defeat them?'

Conn realised that this was an important moment for the people of Mai-dun and for himself. Searching for the right words to try to convey the sense of hopelessness he felt, he looked around the hut. He saw a snail crawling up one of the walls and went to collect it. He laid it on the ground in front of Bannoc. Raising his foot over the creature, he brought his shoe down sharply and smashed the shell and the snail into the earth. 'We have as much chance as that snail,' he said.

Maddoc asked, 'What sort of man is their general? Can we trust what he says?'

'He is a man of such power, like no other I have ever met,' Conn replied. 'He commands hundreds of men with a single word. I believe that if he says he will do something he will do it. If he says he will capture Mai-dun tomorrow he will. If he says no-one need die, then that too will be true.'

The Elders talked quietly amongst themselves. It did not take them long to agree that Bannoc and Maddoc should go to the Roman camp. As they came out of the hut, Julius felt relieved that his mission had been so swiftly successful. 'There is one thing further,' he said to Bannoc. 'The boy must come back with us. The General insists on it.'

Conn tried to protest, but Bannoc cut him short. 'If it is necessary, then it must be so.' He then explained to the rapidly swelling group outside the hut what was happening and asked Garth and Rolf, as the two Elders who remained behind, to tell the people further what had been discussed. He then strode with dignity towards the eastern gate accompanied by Maddoc, Conn and Julius following him.

As the group walked back to the Roman camp flanked by the legionaries, Maddoc moved next to Julius and spoke quietly to him. 'Are you the one who gave the bowl to Conn on the hill?' Julius said this was so and started to explain the circumstances of this but Maddoc cut him short. 'That is all past. It was decided by fate that the two of you should meet. It is important that the two of you be friends. I believe the destiny of my people lies in the hands of this boy and you have been chosen to assist him.' He called Conn forward. 'It is a great thing you have done, Conn. You have shown courage and compassion and you may yet save the people of Mai-dun from much sadness. I believe it is your destiny to serve our people and through you we will come to live in peace with these Romans. This man,' and he indicated Julius, 'is no longer your enemy. We all need you to trust him.' He turned back to Julius. 'Our people need Conn. Look after him well.' Nothing further was said, but the three of them walked back to the Roman camp as companions.

Julius acted as interpreter in the meeting that followed. Vespasian treated Bannoc with respect, but also with great firmness. His terms for the surrender of Mai-dun were simple and not open for negotiation. The leaders would be taken to Rome as prisoners along with one out of every ten of the people. The Romans would select these prisoners. All the defences would be destroyed, never to be rebuilt. The people, except a handful of the old, would have to leave the hilltop and their houses would be burned down. Maddoc could stay as the Teacher for those who remained. Over the next weeks the Roman soldiers would help those who were moved out to rebuild their houses on the flat ground near the River Frome. This community would learn to live at peace with any Romans who stayed behind. If the surrender was agreed by next morning no one need die. He finished with a flourish. 'All this I promise as an officer of the Roman army.'

Bannoc and Maddoc quietly discussed the offer Vespasian had made. Finally Maddoc, turning to the General, spoke. 'I think you are a fair man and Conn tells me you are a man we can trust. I believe Conn is a boy of great insight. We will return to Mai-dun and discuss what you have said with the people. We will let you know our answer by tomorrow morning.'

As the two of them left Vespasian's tent to return to the hillfort, they had to pass through the ranks of the First

Cohort who were drawn up like a silent guard of honour. Neither of them could be in any doubt of the power of the army they were dealing with.

Vespasian, accompanied by Julius and Conn, headed for the hospital tent to visit Carinus. This morning his wrist was more painful and he was running a slight fever, but he sat up when they entered. 'Have they surrendered yet?' was the first thing he asked the General.

Vespasian shook his head. 'Not yet, but they will. I have no doubt that they will talk a while, but they could see that surrender was the only sensible course of action.' He continued, 'When we have destroyed the fortifications at Mai-dun and rebuilt a settlement for them, the legion will continue west. I want Maximus to build a proper legionary fortress here, which I will call Durnovaria. Carinus, I would like you to stay here as the camp commander. With that,' and he pointed at the crippled hand, 'your days as a fighting soldier are over. But you can still serve Rome as her local governor here, and bring these barbarians to an understanding of what it means to belong to Rome's Empire. Send for Romana and the children. Build yourself a villa and settle here in comfort with an estate that can properly support you. You have earned that.'

Carinus, who had been worrying what his future might be, was delighted with what Vespasian proposed. 'Thank you, Sir. I am proud to accept your offer. I have just one request. Can I keep the boy?' He gestured towards Conn. 'Without doubt he saved my life and I must reward him for that.'

Vespasian readily agreed. 'I think he is a young man who will serve you well. If he works alongside you there is a chance that we just might tame this war-like people.' He turned to Julius. 'Tell him what I have decided.' With that he left the hospital tent.

Conn quietly listened to what Julius had to say. He decided to go along for the time being with what he was told, though he did not yet fully understand how the future had been planned for him. He decided to risk a question. 'How will I live?'

Carinus explained what his own new position was to be and told Conn that he would become a member of an important household. 'You will not be a slave. You will be free to leave whenever you want. My job will be to bring peace to this area and you will act as go-between for me with the local leaders.'

Conn remembered what Maddoc had said to him earlier. The offer sounded good to him, but there was just one thing missing. 'Can Morwen come too?' It took Julius a little while to find out about Morwen and then to explain matters to Carinus. But when he understood how important the girl was to Conn he readily agreed that she too could join his household. Carinus sank back on his bed exhausted by all the talking. He asked both of them to leave as he was now tired.

Conn wanted to go back to Mai-dun immediately to see Morwen, but Julius told him from now onwards he would have to stay in the Roman camp. This did not suit Conn at all. Julius had been told to report back to Vespasian and as he left he gave instructions to the guard to keep the boy safe. On the way to his temporary prison Conn wriggled out of the soldier's grasp and started running towards the camp gate. Unfortunately for Conn Goran was on guard duty there. Quite unreasonably the big Slav blamed the boy for the trouble he was in and also for the injury to his friend Novak. At the gates he grabbed hold of Conn and slammed him to the ground, knocking the wind out of him. The two soldiers carried his limp body back to the baggage train and tied him up once more under the wagon.

Chapter 18
END AND BEGINNING

Roman marching camps lacked the superb order and organisation of a legionary fortress. In the marching camp each soldier was responsible both for erecting his own tent and helping to construct a perimeter defence. Every day this defence was strengthened as long as the General decided the legion was to stay in the same place. Vespasian's order that the new fortress at Durnovaria was to become permanent resulted in a flurry of activity in digging ditches and constructing walls. The morning after Bannoc and Maddoc had visited the Roman camp Julius was sent off early by Vespasian to ride to the headquarters at the Reed Pool now called Clavinium, with a dispatch for the soldier in command, a centurion called Quintus Varius. This ordered him to prepare to receive a hundred Celtic prisoners who were to be sent first to Chichester and then on to Rome as soon as possible. Meanwhile Vespasian himself rode out to Mai-dun to accept the anticipated surrender of the Elders. Antonius Drusus, an older officer who had taken over the cohort when Carinus was injured, accompanied him.

When they arrived at Mai-dun, the east gates were immediately opened and Bannoc and Rolf came out. Silda who had volunteered to stay with her husband as a prisoner accompanied Rolf. Bannoc, no longer the Chief of Mai-dun, explained through an interpreter that Garth had run off during the night rather than be a captive of the Romans. Vespasian summoned a centurion. 'These are the leaders of

134

this hillfort. Without them the people will be no problem. Escort them to Clavinium straight away and tell Quintus Varius that I want them kept away from all other prisoners and put on the first ship to Chichester.' He turned to Drusus. 'March the First Cohort through the gates. You know what to do then. Remember my order; for the sake of my honour, no-one must be killed, but the community must be destroyed.' He personally always found the work of sacking villages distasteful and returned to the Roman camp.

Drusus was ideally suited to this task. He was a mean-minded man, embittered by seeing officers such as Carinus promoted above him. His soldiers called him 'Beaky' behind his back because his long nose and hooded eyes made him look like a hawk, but they feared rather than respected him.

Drusus had pleasure in ordering his troops to round up the people and particularly enjoyed selecting those to be sent off as prisoners. He chose 97 more of the youngest and fittest of the adults, as they would be the most use for work as slaves in the farms and households of Rome. It was a sad group that was marched out under escort to join the other three Celtic prisoners already at Clavinium. Drusus then ordered his soldiers to tear down the gates and to assemble work gangs to remove the defences at both gateways that had taken them all winter to construct. Many houses were fired and all but the oldest were driven from the hill. Sticking strictly to Vespasian's promise, no-one was killed, and thus the destruction of the community at Mai-dun was complete.

The following morning Carinus was feeling much better and he sent for Julius and asked what had happened to Conn. Julius promised to find out, and it was an angry and hungry boy he discovered still tied up under the wagon. By now Conn was frantic with worry about what was happening at Mai-dun and Julius secured permission from Carinus to take the boy there immediately and promised to bring him back by nightfall. Julius rode while Conn trotted along beside his horse. They covered the 2 miles to the hillfort rapidly and when they arrived they found the place swarming with Roman soldiers. Most of the huts were smouldering ruins and wretched groups of defeated people sadly picked over the smoking remains. Julius in his years of campaigning had seen the Roman army plunder many settlements, but he was strangely saddened by this sight. Conn noticed Kareth and Gwillam standing forlornly by what was left of their hut. They pathetically appealed to him for help, but he deliberately ignored them, turning his back. He approached another old man who was scraping among the ashes and asked where Rolf and his family were. He was answered with a shrug of shoulders. 'Ask them,' he said, pointing to a group standing by Maddoc's undamaged hut. Conn, followed by Julius, hurried over and found Drusus on horseback shouting instructions at the Teacher, which were obviously not being understood.

'Where are Rolf and his family?' Conn asked Maddoc urgently.

'Rolf and Silda left for the ships yesterday morning. Dirk and Dug have disappeared, but don't worry about them, I'm sure they'll be all right. Those two were born survivors. I am sorry, but Morwen was one of the prisoners selected for Rome.'

Julius, aware how devastatingly this news was to Conn, turned to Drusus and asked about the prisoners.

'I sent the whole lot off yesterday afternoon on Vespasian's orders. They are probably on their way to Chichester already,' Drusus answered. 'You speak their language. Help me tell this old fool to stop getting in my way or he will feel the flat of my sword across his back.'

Julius replied angrily, 'This old fool as you call him is one of the tribal leaders who Vespasian treated with respect. He would require you to do the same.'

Drusus laughed and as he rode off he shouted over his

shoulder, 'Don't forget, he's still a barbarian.'

Maddoc told Julius and Conn about the awful things that had happened the previous day. How, after long discussion, the people had all agreed that surrender was the best course of action. Morwen and the twins had said a tearful goodbye to their parents as they left the hill to hand themselves over to the Romans. No sooner had the soldiers come into the camp than the girl was separated off with the other young adults to form the group that would be sent to Rome as slaves. Before they were marched off she had asked Maddoc to speak to Conn for her. 'She asked me to give you this.' Maddoc handed Conn the small bronze pin they had found together and which the boy had fastened to her dress such a short time ago. The boy gazed at it with utter misery.

'I promised Rolf I would look after her. I promised him,' Conn said with tears streaming down his face. He turned to Julius. 'What will happen to her?'

Julius explained to the distraught boy that there were thousands of slaves in Rome, and many of them had pleasant lives in wealthy Roman households. He was uncomfortably aware that many others had terrible lives working in the mines and in the fields and the fate of a young female slave was not something he cared to share with Conn.

Julius was moved by Conn's grief and thought perhaps now he could make amends for his earlier betrayal. 'Come on, Conn. Let's see if there is anything we can do. It may not be too late.' He pulled the boy up behind him on the horse and rode swiftly out of Mai-dun.

Conn had never been on a horse before and he clung on as they moved quickly across the Ridgeway past Beacon Hill. From the summit they could see a Roman galley crabbing across the bay, moving eastwards. Julius feared that Morwen might well be one of its passengers. They hurried on and soon reached the port. There was a great deal of activity and some confusion in the harbour at Clavinium, but Julius used his rank to find out where

Quintus might be. It turned out that he was away from the headquarters hut, but a centurion told Julius that half the prisoners had already sailed with the morning tide, and the remainder were being kept in one of the half-empty storehouses. Julius followed by Conn hurried to where they were directed. One of the guards let them in and through the gloom Conn saw many faces that he recognised, all looking stunned and frightened. He found Ox and asked him if he knew where Morwen was. His friend smiled briefly at Conn, but looked strained and scared. 'I think she's here somewhere,' Ox said. 'I saw her last night.' Getting increasingly frantic Conn continued to search the dark shed. At last, sitting frightened and miserable in a corner, he saw Morwen at the same time as she looked up and saw him. With a cry she scrambled to her feet and rushed into his arms, sobbing. Conn held her, unable to speak for relief that he had found her. She explained that Rolf and Silda had been shipped out last night and that her group was due to leave at the next turn of the tide that evening.

Conn, continuing to hold her tightly, explained the position he had been offered in Carinus's household. 'He has promised there could be a place for you too. Together we can help those of our people who are left to live at peace with the Romans. Will you come and live with us?'

'Do you mean we would be wed?' she asked.

'Of course. You know I've always wanted to marry you and when we buried Huw your father specially asked me to look after you.' There was no need for her to answer as she buried her face again in his shoulder, quietly crying with relief.

Julius, who had been watching and listening to all this, interrupted. 'There is just one problem, Conn. I promised Carinus that I would take you back to the legionary camp this evening. Morwen, however, is a prisoner of Rome and is supposed to be getting on a ship this evening. I have no authority to release her.'

Conn begged him to do something, and Julius agreed that he would try. He dragged Conn away from Morwen, telling him that her freedom was only possible if Quintus, the officer in charge of Clavinium, would agree.

Centurion Quintus, who had met Julius the previous day, was back in his headquarters. Although a conscientious officer he was a cautious man and always careful to follow orders from his superiors. When Julius explained the position he shook his head sadly. 'I'm sorry, Tribune. I would like to help, but you yourself brought me orders yesterday from the General to send 100 prisoners to Chichester and then onwards to Rome. I sent 50 yesterday and I will send the other 50 later today. There is nothing I can do about it unless I get a further order from Vespasian.'

Julius knew there wasn't time to ride back to see Vespasian and to catch the galley before it sailed. He looked at Conn's expectant face, aware that if he did nothing he would dash all his hopes. He pleaded with Quintus to change his mind, but the Centurion shook his head. 'I can't do it, Tribune. If it was my choice I would, but I can't risk disobeying instructions. It would take an order from the Emperor himself to go against what the General has said. You don't have the authority.'

Quintus's words triggered a memory of an earlier conversation he had had with Maximus when the fortress at Lake Camp was first being built. Julius felt for the leather pouch he always carried around his waist. He opened the clasp and his hand dived inside. He brought out the letter Maximus had given to him before his trip to Gaul and which had lain forgotten since then.

'But I do have imperial authority,' he said. 'Here is a letter signed by Claudius himself. I will take the girl back. You will have only 99 prisoners to send to Rome.'

ABOUT THE AUTHOR

David Macpherson taught history for 15 years and has published articles on local history in *The Marshwood Vale*. *Defenders of Mai-dun* is his first novel, inspired by frequent visits to Maiden Castle to walk his dog and to the Dorset County Museum. David has worked for the United Nations running a refugee camp for Tibetans in Nepal, and for the charity 'Britain Nepal Medical Trust', responsible for tuberculosis and leprosy control in East Nepal. He now works as a youth magistrate, as well as writing more novels set in Dorset.

Photo by Sue Macpherson ARPS

SOME FACTS BEHIND THE STORY

The great archaeologist Sir Mortimer Wheeler, who excavated Maiden Castle in the 1930s, wrote a breathtaking account of the bloody Roman assault, but Niall Sharples' dig in 1985 found little evidence to support this idea. As there are no signs of destruction of the hillfort, it would suggest the inhabitants surrendered peacefully. Almost no written record of the Durotriges tribe who lived in Dorset in the Iron Age exists – apart from a marker stone from Hadrian's Wall in the museum at Chester's Fort which reads: '*C DVRTRG LENDINESIS*' [The Century of the Durotriges from Lindinis (Ilchester) have made this]. Roman records of Vespasian's invasion, largely from Tacitus's *Histories*, are also vague.

In the book, Vespasian, Titus and Publius Maximus are all accurately portrayed. I have created all other Romans and all the Durotriges characters. The following objects can be found in the Dorset County Museum:

- Huw's skeleton with the ballista bolt still stuck in his spine
- The skeleton of Bran with the skull wound clearly visible
- The Samian bowl Julius gave to Conn that was buried with Huw
- Bannoc's drinking cup made of black burnished pottery

- Maddoc's incense dish
- Thousands of slingshot which I have called chesils
- A replica of Carinus's gravestone (the original is in the porch of St George's Church, Fordington), with the following inscription:

CARINO	Carinus
CIVI ROM	citizen of Rome
ANN L	aged 50
RUFINUS ET	and Rufinus,
CARINA ET	Carina
AVITA FILI EIUS	and Avita his children
ET ROMANA UXOR	and his wife Romana

The legionary fort called Lake Farm, discovered near Wimborne when the town by-pass was being built, I have called *Lake Camp*, the Roman port at Hamworthy I call *Lagoon Harbour* and the Roman harbour at Radipole is *Reed Pool*. The line of the Roman road from Weymouth to Dorchester can be seen as it passes the Old Ship Inn at Upwey, and the roads Alexis helped to construct are clearly marked on Ordnance Survey maps. The Iron Age hillforts of Maiden Castle, Hod Hill and Badbury Rings speak for themselves.

WHERE TO LEARN MORE

Maiden Castle is an English Heritage site, 2 miles SW of Dorchester

Hod Hill, 4 miles NW of Blandford on the A350

Badbury Rings, 4 miles NE of Wimborne

New Barn Field Centre, Bradford Peverell, 2 miles NW of Dorchester

Thorncombe Woods, near Higher Bockhampton, where a Roman road has been uncovered stretching approx. 1 mile through the woods into Puddletown Forest

Maumbury Rings, Dorchester

Dorchester Roman Villa

Dorset County Museum, High West Street, Dorchester

The Romans by Professor Bill Putnam

The Romans in Dorset by Maureen Putnam (Key Stage Level 2)

ACKNOWLEDGEMENTS

An early draft of the story was vetted by the late Professor Bill Putnam. I would also like to thank Jo Scott, David Miller and Kikki Schaffer for their help and encouragement. Special thanks also to Keith Whittock for his map and line drawing.

OTHER ROVING PRESS TITLES

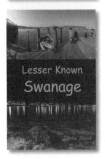

Roving
Press